IT BEGINS

WITH

GOODBYE

R.S.

JAMES

Copyright

It Begins with Goodbye
Copyright © 2019 R.S. James

Edited: Nikki Reeves of Southern Sweetheart Author
and Book Services
Cover Design: Tracie Douglas of Dark Water Covers
Photographer: Dawn Chance of Zenyx Photography
Models: Julie E Mick Schalm
Formatting: Jaime Russell
Chapter Header Designs: Torrie Robles

R.S. James

author.

Acknowledgements

First, I want to thank God. Second, I want to thank my husband and both my kids I love you most best always forever times infinity and beyond. I want to thank Jaime Russell and Avelyn Paige for your unwavering support. I love you both.

R.S. James begins with readers, southern sweethearts editing and Tracie Douglas at Dark Water Covers and the wonderful and beautiful Julie Mick Schalm for honoring me with your photo on my cover. Thank you to one of my favorite authors Chelle Bliss for allowing me to use the copyrighted name of her Men of Inked shirt.

R.S. James

Table of Contents

Chapter One

Claire

Can this day get any worse?

Today is supposed to be my first day off, after working the last sixty days straight, but now, I've been called into cover a shift at a hospital in the next county. One of their emergency room nurses has been in a car accident, sending her into labor three weeks early. Today, also happens to be my fifteenth wedding anniversary.

We live in Reading, Michigan, and the main reason I've been working so much is, so I can afford to buy Colton the Alaska hunting trip he has always wanted. Our children, Carly and Carson, are staying with friends tonight. I've been trying to call Colton, ever since I found out that I'm needed here tonight, but he isn't answering. I left a message, and I hope he's not too pissed.

When I pull up, the place is packed. All the bays are full, and the waiting room is wall to wall with people. *This is going to be fun!* Yep, another twelve-hour shift, here I come. Walking through the doors of the locker room, I type out a text to the kids, letting them know the change in plans, where I am, and what time I get off tomorrow. All the while, I can't get my mind off of not being able to get a hold of my husband. I have a strange feeling something has been going on lately because Colton has been so moody and withdrawn. I try pushing it from my mind, so I can get some work done.

Standing behind the counter typing up a chart, I hear a familiar voice talking. *Wait, what's going on? Are the kids, okay? Did Colton come to surprise me?* My questions are answered, when I see him walking towards the bay area. He is holding a woman's hand, like he held mine in the beginning, but hasn't since the kids. In that moment, I know I've been right all along. He hasn't been faithful to me, and I'm beyond

8

hurt and furious. I have never felt such hate in my life. Not only for my so-called "husband," but also for my twin sister, the woman he's with. *What the actual fuck?*

I stay behind the counter, until the doctor comes back, telling me which labs he wants to be ordered for the patient in bay four. It also happens to be exactly where my husband is currently holding my sister. I get all my supplies and head in there. I hear a gasp, so I look up. "Oh, hey. What's going on, guys?"

"What are you doing here? I thought you had the weekend off," Colton asks, sounding pissed off.

"Well, if you had listened to your voicemail, then you would know what's going on." They just watch me not knowing what's going to happen, and honestly, neither do I. However, I have two kids that need me, so I'm going to do my job right now.

"So, the doctor has ordered some lab work, as well as a urine sample. I'm going to put an IV in to get you some fluids, and a phlebotomist will be in to draw some blood to take to the lab downstairs. We'll be back with the results, as soon as they come in. Okay?"

Again, there's no response, so I get my gloves on. "I'm sorry, sir. I'm going to need you to let go of your wife's arm, so I can get in there and get the IV started for the doctor." He finally lets her arm go. "Isn't there another nurse that can do this?" Colton whispers.

"I'm sorry if I have made you angry sir, but the doctor needs these to help make a proper diagnosis. I'll only be a second, and then you can be with your wife again."

"Cut the shit, Claire. You know she's not my wife."

"Well yes, Colton, I do know that. I also know that today is our fifteenth wedding anniversary, and I got called into a different hospital to cover for another nurse. When I got here, I see my husband walking in, holding my twin sister, as if she is his wife. Right this second, I can't be the hurt wife or sister. I need to be a professional and get this IV

10

started. So please, let's make this as painless as possible for everyone, okay?"

"Well Claire, it does look bad, since we've been sleeping together for the past eighteen months," Clarissa responds snotty. I nod my head, understanding all the looks and whispers lately between them. Once again, I have been played for a fool. Well, that's fine, but I'm done. No more pathetic Claire. I wish I could say this is the first time he's cheated, but sadly, it's not. I wish I could say I was strong enough to leave him the first time, but again, that's not the case.

They both just look at each other, as I walk out to the doctor, asking him to come into the room with me for a minute. We walk back in, and I tell him the story, and he watches, as I take the blood. "I have no problem treating her, nor do I have a problem being professional. I merely brought you in for their comfort."

Colton looks down, "Well, it does kind of look bad. Don't you agree?"

"Colton, what I think right now has no reflection on how I treat patients, or how I do my job. And no, it doesn't just look bad. It looks like a disaster, but I'm sure you know what and who you want, so that's all that matters." Turning, I face the doctor, "Doctor Anderson, the blood has been drawn and sent to the lab. She is hooked up to the monitors, an IV has been put in, and her vitals are stable. As soon as I get the results, I'll let you know."

With a nod, I'm out the door, as if the hounds of hell are at my feet. I make it down the hall to the lady's room, and then hurry inside, as I turn the lock on the door. Leaning against it, I start to question everything. Am I hurt? Fuck yeah, but not as much as I thought I would be. Am I going to let them know that they have destroyed my self-esteem and self-respect? No! I'm going to go out there and be the best nurse I can be to not only them, but to all my patients. I'm also going to pretend that my world isn't crashing in around me.

I walk to the sink, splashing cold water on my face. It's a good thing I don't wear makeup because I would scare everyone, after just washing it off. My phone vibrates, and I look at it, seeing a message from Carly.

Carly: I love you, Mom. Have a good night and stay safe. Michelle and I are back and in for the night. See you tomorrow!

One from Carson comes in next.

Carson: I love you, Mom. Have a great night, and I hope it's slow. Maybe you and Dad can go out tomorrow night. Carly and I will be fine. See you tomorrow."

Man, I have the best kids ever. I send them a quick text, saying I love them and will see them tomorrow as well. No need to let them know that their dad and aunt may be having a baby together, and I'm getting a divorce. I remember what my symptoms were, when I was pregnant, and I also know this isn't her first time being pregnant. She hasn't been able to carry a baby full term yet.

My pager goes off, letting me know the lab work is done and waiting for me. Well, it's time to face the music. This might get interesting. Leaving the restroom, I make my way to the counter, as the doctor asks again, if I can handle this. Nodding my head, he looks at me with questions all over his face. With a sigh, I begin to explain what is occurring. "I can remove you and put someone else on the case, if you would like." He says with sympathy.

"I have been nothing but professional thus far, so I will continue to be. However, when my shift is over, and I get home, that will be a totally different story." I smile at him, while my eyes are burning, trying to hold the tears back.

I stare at the chart in Doctor Anderson's hand, which has my sister's name on it. He slides me the file, which I appreciate, because I don't want to hear the news with them. I open the folder with shaking hands, and then I hurry up and close it. Taking a few small breaths, I say, "Let's do this."

Walking to the door, I knock, as Colton says, "Come on in." When he sees me, he starts speaking right away, "Well, does she have food poisoning, like I said?"

I smile, "I can't you give the results. The doctor has, too." My voice shakes. "I have another patient to check on, so I'll be back." Walking out of the cubical, I stand next to the door and listen.

The doctor begins to speak, "Well, looks like you're pregnant, and I brought the portable ultrasound machine, so I can give you an estimated due date. Let's see, if we can find your little bundle of joy. Now, you're going to need to follow up with your OBGYN and set up your regular appointments." Not long after, the swooshing sound begins. "What the hell is that?" My sister asks, sounding a bit panicky.

"Just relax. That is your baby's heartbeat, and it looks like you are about 8 weeks, making your due date somewhere around May 21st. I will get you a prescription for prenatal vitamins and folic acid, but just remember to call and follow up with the doctor. I can also give you a list with phone numbers, if you would like?"

"No, we can handle this. We will use the same one Claire used with the kids, right babe?"

"Okay, I'll have Claire bring your discharge paperwork in, as soon as it's done."

Walking back in the room, I have my mask in place. I cannot believe I shared a womb with this bitch. Everyone's eyes are solely on me, as Colton speaks up first "Claire I never..." He looks to Clarissa, before speaking again, "We never meant for this to happen. It was only supposed to be once." He quickly looks away, so I instantly know he's lying.

"Yeah, once a day, unless we could find time for it more often." Clarissa snottily replies.

I hand the paperwork to Colton, and as I'm doing so, he asks, "What time do you get off? I'd like a chance to explain things to you. I didn't want you to find out this way." I'm standing here looking at the two people, who are supposed to love me, and they are the same ones that have destroyed that love. *Now, they want to explain?* Fuck that shit.

I can't hold it in anymore. "Oh? Were you going to explain over dinner tonight for our fifteenth wedding anniversary, or just hope the stupid little wife never finds out, so you can have your cake and eat it, too? Well, I'm so sorry I've ruined your fairy tale."

Turning to walk away, he grabs my arm just as the doctor calls me, letting me know we have an ambulance coming in. "This isn't done, and we will be talking." He says, gritting his teeth.

"Go to hell," I say, walking away. I'm actually able to finish my shift without any sign that my world just changed. I'm proud of myself for holding my head up high all night.

Standing in the staff lounge, I hear the door open behind me. "Wow, I'm impressed with your behavior! I don't know many women would've been that calm during that, and then, you went to the trauma, like you hadn't just had your heart ripped out. I hope to see you over here more often." Doctor Anderson says, putting his hand on my shoulder.

I smile, giving him my thanks, when in my head, I'm screaming, "Thank you so much for enjoying my world crashing around me, and I'm so glad that I could help you out with the entertaining portion of this evening. God! Are all men total assholes, or do I have a beam that attracts them?" I feel bad because I know Dr. Anderson isn't trying to be an asshole. It's just me tonight.

As I make my way to my car, I see Colton standing there. "Man, can't I catch a freaking break? I was hoping I wouldn't have to deal with him, until I got some sleep. No such luck." I mutter to myself.

"So, how mad are you?"

"Excuse me?" I look at him, like he has just sprouted two heads.

"Okay, I know it's bad, but it's not totally our fault."

"Oh yes, that's right cause your dick just accidentally got hard, and then landed in her vagina. You're so right. It's totally not your fault at all." I pause for a minute, taking in a deep breath. "Look Colton, I'm tired, and I just want to go home, get in my bed, and sleep. Can we maybe schedule this for some time tomorrow, or maybe I'll just file for divorce, and we can just be done." He opens his mouth, like he's about to say something, but I stop him. "No, don't say anything, because there is no coming back from this. I forgave you both times that I had proof you were cheating, but not this time. I'm so done!"

I walk past him, and then get in my car, starting it up. I roll my window down, testing to see if he will play into this. "Hey, can I see your keys?" The idiot actually hands them to me, and I take my car key and the house key off, and then put his truck key from my keychain onto his. Handing them back to him, I smile, "Good luck in life, asshole." With a wave, I'm off and headed home.

It Begins with Goodbye

I rock out to Three Days Grace and Seether on my way. *I love music.* You can always tell my moods by the music I listen to. Yup, I'm pissed off, so the harder and louder the better. I get home at two forty-five in the morning. Well, it's Saturday morning now, so I'll have to wait to call the lawyer, until Monday morning. What the hell, I'll just call now and leave a message. Maybe he will stop by the office or something. After leaving a message and taking a shower, the day is catching up with me, and I barely make it to bed, before I'm sound asleep.

******

I wake around four hours later with my phone ringing, and I answer with a groggy, "Hello."

"Yes, I'm looking for a Claire Mercier?"

"Yes, this is she. How can I help you?"

"Good morning, Mrs. Mercier. This is Morgan Bliss, the divorce attorney, you called earlier this morning. I'm just returning your phone call."

"Oh, yes. Sorry, I wasn't expecting to get a call back, until at least Monday. I found out last night that my husband has been cheating on me with my twin sister, and they are having a baby together, so I'd like for this to be over, as quick as possible."

"Wow, it sounds like you have had a rough night. Can you meet at our offices today around eight-thirty to go over some things?"

"Umm, I'm sorry. I'm a nurse, and I worked the night shift. I was actually asleep, when you called. I'll need more than an hour. Can we make it for nine-thirty?"

Why in the hell is an attorney, meeting clients on a Saturday morning, and not charging an obscene amount of money to do that?

"Yes, ma'am. See you then."

When I hear the click, I jump out of bed and run to the shower, taking the fastest one ever. Getting out and drying off, I apply lotion, and then head to my bedroom, grabbing panties, a bra, a pair of blue

21

jeans, and my *Men of Inked* t-shirt. I go in the bathroom, noticing I look a little worn down, but a girls gotta do what a girls gotta do. So, I put a little concealer on, brush my hair and teeth, spray myself with body spray, and head to the lawyer's office. As I'm backing out of my driveway, my phone rings. *Fantastic, it's my mom.* I sync the call, and then answer, "Hey Mom. What's up this morning?"

"Claire, what on earth is going on? Clarissa and Colton just told me, and then they posted on social media, that they are pregnant and in a relationship. Are you okay? You're not going to do something stupid, are you?"

"I haven't even told the kids, and they are blabbing it all over social media?" I shriek, knowing my kids are going to see it. "What do you mean, am I going to do something stupid? I'm going to see the lawyer and get a divorce. They can have each other. So no, I'm not doing anything stupid."

"Well, I can't say that I blame you. I've told you from the beginning that you deserved so much better than him. I'm so sorry you're going through this. I understand why you took him back the first time, but after that, I was confused."

"Mom, I just wanted the fairy tale, but now, I see he is not that. I just need to be the strong parent for my kids. I don't want Carly to think this kind of behavior is okay, because it's not. I also don't want Carson to think of women as objects that you can use as you want. I want him to respect women. And Mom, I'm so tired of pretending that I'm happy, or that we have a good marriage. I just want to be happy. I'm sad that, after fifteen years, it's over. However, I don't regret what we had, because it gave me my babies, and it has taught me what I will and will not accept in future relationships. I need you to understand I will not be attending any family functions, if Clarissa is there. As far as I'm concerned, she is dead to me."

"I understand, but she is also my daughter, as much as you are."

"I know Mom, but she had sex with my husband and has been for the last eighteen months. And to top it off, I had to learn about this on our fifteenth wedding anniversary, while being professional, during the whole thing. I truly hope she is what makes him happy, and they can be together, but I'm not sure I can forgive this. It's too big, and I'm so sorry it hurts you. I can come over early, later, or even the day before or the day after whatever is occurring, but don't ask me to join, when they will be there. No, I will not help with a baby shower, nor will I be getting them gifts or letting them use my furniture. I'm done with them both."

"What about Carly and Carson? What are you going to tell them? You know Carly loves Clarissa, and Carson loves his father."

"I'm not sure, because if the kids read it on social media or a friend contacts them, there might be a lot of questions that I don't have the answers to. I don't want them to hate their dad. However, I will not lie to them. Okay, Mom. I'm at the lawyer's office, so I'll call you later. Please don't tell them you talked to me. I just need a day or so. Maybe the kids and I will come get you tomorrow, and then take you out for dinner just the four of us. Sound good?"

"Sure, baby girl. If you need me, I'm always here for you. I love you!"

"Thanks, Momma. I love you, too!"

Taking a deep breath, I look into the rear-view mirror, giving myself a pep talk. "Is this the right thing to do? Yes. Does it hurt? Yes. But will I be okay after? Yes, I most certainly will. Come on! Go got this, Claire."

Colton

I'm such a fuck up. I don't know why I listened to Clarissa, when she said I didn't need to worry about a condom, and that she was on birth control. Yes, I've messed around before, but Claire has always forgiven me. I took Clarissa to the other hospital, thinking Claire would be at home, waiting for me for our anniversary dinner. Instead, not only did my wife find out I've been fucking her sister, but also, that said sister is pregnant with my child. The twins are almost done with school, and it appears I will be starting all over. *Fuck my life. I didn't want any more kids.*

As I waited for Claire to get out of work, I tried to come up with a reason good enough as to why I cheated. Then, I thought to myself what would be an okay reason for *her* to cheat, and there isn't any. I could try and lie, but once the child is born, it will backfire. That is also one promise I've never broken. I've evaded, distracted, and flat out ignored questions from her, but I've never lied. I have no reason for why I cheated. I mean, anything I have ever wanted Claire has given me. I guess it's the thrill of having what is forbidden. I'm forbidden from any and all other woman, and they are to me.

The last time Claire caught me cheating I caught an STD. Thankfully, it was curable, but that should have been a wakeup call, yet it wasn't. She has just been working so many hours, but I can't blame her or even be angry at her. She doesn't tell others our problems, and a lot of my buddie's bitch, because their wives are always tossing their problems around to their friends. Not Claire, though. Hell, the kids don't even know what I've done. I know how to play mind games with Claire too. She listens to everything I say, and I know she's upset right now, but she will see that this is all for the best.

Here is the real kicker I'm not sorry, and I can almost guarantee that I'll cheat again. Maybe not with Clarissa, but it will happen again. It's almost like I'm addicted to sex, and I need the thrill of it. One of my favorite things is sex in public with the fear of getting caught. I just can't stop though. I always need someone to take care of me, which is why I've stayed with Clarissa so long. Too bad, she can't satisfy everything.

Claire

Squaring my shoulders, I get out of the car, walking up to the doors. I open one, as I step inside, but there is no one at the reception desk. I wait a minute, and then holler a quick, "Hello?"

Walking down the hallway, I see a door ajar with a light on, so I head in that direction. As I get closer, I see a gentleman, in a red polo shirt with black framed glasses and thick black hair, sitting at a desk. I knock on the door, and his head whips up. All the breath leaves my lungs. Damn, I haven't felt the wind knocked out of me, since I fell down the stairs, when I was eight! *He's gorgeous.* He has beautiful chocolate eyes, and I seriously feel like I gained five pounds just looking at them. Being married, I've never really looked at anyone else like that, but now, I can truly appreciate his beauty.

He smiles, "Hello. Can I help you?"

"My name is Claire Mercier, and I have an appointment with an attorney to start my divorce."

"Ah yes, I'm Morgan. I was hoping that was you and not some random person selling something. Come on in and have a seat. Can I get you anything to drink, or maybe something to snack on?" We shake hands, and I hold onto his hand a little bit longer than I should, but this man is breathtaking.

"No, I'm okay. I just want to get this started and over, as quickly as possible."

"Okay, so start at the beginning, and tell me what caused you to end your marriage? Also, is there any way it can be saved?"

The first part of our conversation starts with what has transpired in the past twenty hours or so.

Next, I explain our past, and how he has cheated twice before that I know of.

"We have done couples counselling and individual therapy, and I'm just done now. There is no saving our marriage, because I can't save it alone, and he doesn't care enough to try, so here I am."

"Okay, so you, and I'm sorry, what's his name?"

"Colton Mercier."

"Right. Do you and Mr. Mercier have any children together?"

"Yes, a set of twins, Carly and Carson. They are sixteen. They'll be seventeen in April, and then they will graduate from high school next year."

"Do you own properties together? Houses, condos, apartments, or anything like that."

"I know we own the house we are currently living in. However, it's apparent my husband has been living a double life, so to be honest with you, I have no idea, if he went out and bought other stuff. I can tell you this though I don't want anything, except the kids. I'll find us a new place to live. Maybe that's my pride talking right now, but I want nothing to do with him, and I definitely don't need anything from him."

"Okay, but the judge is going to look at these items, and if he is keeping things from you, then it's going to look so much worse for him, which is exactly we want. Do you guys own any vehicles together?"

"I own my car, he owns his truck, and we bought the kids their own vehicles. They are in my name, until they are eighteen, and they also have jobs to cover the insurance and gas money. Again, other than that, no idea. I'm so sorry. I feel like this is a recurring nightmare."

"Claire, please don't apologize because you've done nothing wrong. You actually did everything right. Most women wouldn't have taken him back, after the first-time he was caught cheating, let alone the second. Plus, he's still doing it now. I just need you to understand that, if you ever decide you don't want to follow through with the divorce, that's fine cause you're the boss. It's whatever you want."

"I'm divorcing him. No doubt in my mind." I say matter of fact.

"Okay, so talk to me like I'm your friend. Tell me the story of Claire and Colton. How it began, the good, bad, and the ugly. I want to know everything. No matter how small you feel it is please just tell me." I take a deep breath, and then let my mind go back to the beginning.

"We met, when our cousins got married, and we were both just guests. I spotted him across the church, and he was breathtaking. I was fresh out of high school, so I felt as if I had the world at my hands. I had planned on attending college because I wanted to be a doctor and help heal people. I kind of went in that direction, but I took the scenic route. When we had the twins, I refused to get married just because I was pregnant, and there had to be a better reason. So, the kids were around one, when we finally decided to get married." I pause for a second because I know it's about to get deep.

"The first time I found out he had cheated was when his mom called me, asking to bring the kids over, so she could visit them. I took them over, and she asked me to go into Colton's old room to get something. When I walked in, there he was with his old girlfriend, and they never stopped. I turned around, picked the kids up, and then left. I don't know if his mom knew or not, but at the time, I was already suffering badly from depression, and I hated my body. He told me that it was my fault, because I didn't have the *same tight body* anymore, so what was I supposed to do? I believed him that it was my fault, and that he wasn't attracted to my post pregnancy body. So, I started to walk, as much as I could, pushing the kids in a double stroller versus driving. Not long after that happened we started counselling." I pause for a minute, trying to get myself together, before I continue.

"Everything was good for a while, until he did it again. The second time I had to take the kids to the doctor for shots, and his mom called me asking me to go check on him at work. Apparently, he had gotten into an argument with someone, so he called her. When I got there, he was letting some girl go down on him. I threw him out, and he was gone for a year. During that whole time, he only came to see the kids once. They cried after he left, and he of course, shed his crocodile tears begging for forgiveness, saying he wanted his family back. I gave in and gave him another chance. I know it was cliché of me thinking he would change, but after a while, I finally realized a zebra can't change its stripes." He's staring at me now with a look of sadness, but I turn my head, continuing on.

"I continued with counselling, and that's where I met Molly and Frank. Frank is gayer than Elton John, and Molly is someone who needed help at the time to fight her demons. We all just clicked, and they are the best friends that I could ever ask for.

They helped me realize I was more than a mom or a wife. I'm a woman who still has hopes and dreams, and I deserve for them to come true. Late one night, I heard a song on the radio that became my life's theme song "Stay" by Sugarland. It made me want to do better things." This makes me smile a bit, while also reminding me of my dreams.

"So, I went back to college and got my nursing degree in eighteen months, and Colton was pissed. He wanted me to depend on him emotionally, mentally, and financially. We fought a lot over me going to school. He would say, *"If you truly love me, you don't need to go to college or work."* If I hadn't been in counselling, I wouldn't have finished. I was so used to doing what he wanted, and I almost caved in several times, but Molly would remind me that I had dreams too, and if he loved me, then he would support them no matter what."

"Then, we had another bad fight, when I got the job at the hospital. That was when I worked only

Monday through Friday. No holidays and no weekends, but that still didn't matter. He felt like I should stay home all the time and have dinner on the table, when he got home. He also expected a lot of out of me sexually, too. One night I was home with the kids, and we had been in bed for about two hours, when he came home drunk. I could smell the alcohol on him, as soon as he came in the bedroom. I pretended to be asleep, as he stripped his clothes off. He mumbled under his breath the whole time, then he ripped the blankets off, and pulled my pants off, shoving roughly inside of me. I cried out in pain, but he just whispered into my ear, *"Shut up! This is your job, as my wife, to give me pleasure."* I begged him to stop, but the more I begged the rougher he became. I honestly only stayed with him because I felt like I owed the kids a home with both parents. I think in a lot of ways I was there physically, but not emotionally or mentally. I know it's considered rape, but he said it was the woman's duty, and that no judge or jury would withhold this from the husband.

By this point, I was pretty much done, but I did still love him, as crazy as that sounds."

I pause for a minute again, and he doesn't say a word, letting me process everything. "So, when the position for a trauma nurse came up, I applied for it, and then I got it. I was so happy, but he was so pissed that he pushed me down the stairs. There is a report at the ER, and I can get that for you." I watch, as Morgan makes notes on a yellow pad. He still doesn't interrupt me with words, but I can hear the small noises and read his face. It's nice being able to bare my soul to someone.

"I fractured my left arm and broke three ribs, which also punctured my lung. I was in the hospital for eight days. That's the one and only time he hit me. I did press charges, and he spent the night in jail, before his mom bailed him out. That happened a few months ago, and I also took my name off his accounts and started my own. I tried for an order of protection, but the judge didn't feel I was in danger, even though I had just been in the hospital due to him." I know it's because his family has strong ties with the judge, and that's why it wasn't granted.

"When the judge denied me, I started to plan my new life away from him, after the twins' graduation. I've been looking for a new place to live, changed my life insurance policies, and made the kids my power of attorney. My will states that they get everything divided up equally between the two of them. The officer that I dealt with felt bad about the order of protection, so he checks in with me weekly. So yes, he cheated, but I was already in the process of leaving, which is why I think I'm not hurt as bad as I should be."

"What was it like, when you and Colton would go out with friends or family? Tell me about his behavior." Morgan asks, and I take a deep breath to calm my nerves. I didn't realize I had so much frustration, hurt, and anger pent up inside of me. I guess it's true what they say that love is blind. Looking back on all of this, I should have left him many years ago.

It Begins with Goodbye

"When our friends would call to invite me or both of us to go out to dinner, play cards, or go to a movie, we could agree, but when the time came, he was full of excuses. His normal ones were I'm tired, we don't have the money, or we don't have anyone to watch the kids. I wanted to give our marriage one more chance, giving it one hundred percent, and that's why I worked a full two months straight, so I could afford to get him the hunting trip to Alaska that he has been wanting. It was going to be the honeymoon we never had." I pause for a minute because this is where everything changed in the last several hours.

"Then I find out he has been cheating with my twin. When I saw them together, it finally just came to me. I'm never going to be enough for him, and he is going to always do these things to me. My heart hurts for my two kids, and the innocent baby who's going to be born into such chaos." I wipe a lone tear that falls from the corner of my eye.

"So, I made the decision I would not enable him anymore, so here I am. I just want this to be over.

I don't want money, the house, or alimony. I want him to take care of his children and help them with college. They are old enough to drive themselves to see him, so there's no way that I have to see him again, except for functions for the kids." Feeling the adrenaline drain from me, I ask, "Can we continue this later in the week?"

"Of course. I have enough to get started, and it will be early in the week, when I get a hold of you. If you have anything else or need anything, please feel free to call me. I've put my personal information on this card for you to put my info into your phone, so I know you have it. If you decide to rent a place, please call me with the address."

"Thank you so much for all of your help. Do you happen to know about how much will this cost me?"

"Let's just worry about that later."

"I really need to do this on my own, so please just tell me."

"Six hundred dollars is the retainer, but I'll take anything you can put down to start. It's also going to depend on how long of a process it is. I know you want it done quickly, however, we have no way of knowing, if he is going to drag it out. So again, we will figure it out, when the time comes."

"I have three hundred and fifty-dollars cash, right now. If you need the full amount, I can go get it."

"No, I can't accept any money today, because the person who usually handles the billing isn't in, until Monday. How about we just settle, when this is done. It won't be a problem, I promise."

"Don't you have to take money from me, so everything is lawyer-client privilege or whatever?"

"No, you're my client. Which means, anything and everything you say to me is between you and me no matter what, unless I need to get any help from my colleagues. That's the only exception."

"Okay, as long you're sure." My tone is one of pure confusion. This kinda feels almost too good to be true.

"Yes, I'm positive. Thank you for coming in, and also, thank you for choosing us as your attorneys."

"I didn't choose an us. I chose you."

"If someone hires a law firm, then you hire everyone that works there, and not just one lawyer. We have law students, lawyers, and secretaries working here." I must look a bit anxious because he adds, "I promise to do as much as I can without involving anyone else. Is that, okay?"

"Yes, thank you. I work Monday from noon until midnight, but I'll be able to check my phone throughout the day. Again, thanks for coming in on your Saturday morning off. I hope you have a good rest of your weekend." We walk out of the building together, and I go to my car, as he locks up.

I start my car, and then reach over to I get my phone out of my bag. *Holy shit.* I have fifteen missed calls and five text messages from Colton.

Colton: Where are you?

Colton: Claire, we need to talk.

Colton: She doesn't mean anything to me. Please, don't do this to us or the kids.

Colton: If I can't have you bitch, no one will.

Colton: I mean it Claire. Don't do anything stupid.

I jump, when there is a knock on my window, and I look up, seeing it's Morgan.

"You okay? Well, that's kind of an oxymoron, isn't it? I can clearly see you're not, so please tell me what happened."

"Well, I have fifteen missed calls from my soon to be ex, and I haven't gotten to listen to the voicemails. There are also five text messages. Should I forward them to you?"

"Let's go back inside and listen to the voicemails. That way I can record them, and I'll have you send me screenshots of the text messages just in case we need to use them."

"Okay." Just then my phone starts ringing, flashing Wolverine Rental.

"Oh, hang on this is the rental company my friend and co-worker Jaime told me about. They are very affordable and try to meet all of your requests. They have a listing that I called to make an appointment to see." I stop talking to him, and then answer the phone. "Hello. Yes, this is Claire. I received your number from Jaime, who I work with at the hospital, and I was looking on your website and saw a rental on North Tommy Road, and I would like some more information on that please."

I listen, as a girl named Ava, gives me the details about the rent, security deposit, and all the ins and outs of the property. "Will I be able to see it today?"

"Yes, ma'am. Is one o'clock, okay?"

"Yes, I can be there. Can you give me the number of the house, so I know which one it is?"

"124 North Tommy Road."

"Thank you so much, and I'll see you soon." I hang up, and then get out of the car.

Walking into the office, I forward the screenshots of the text messages to Morgan, as he gets a tape recorder, and then begins talking into it. "This is Morgan Bliss with Claire Mercier on August 22, 2016. Claire came into the office this morning. She was in here for about forty-five minutes, and her husband called several times. Here are the voicemails from Mr. Colton Mercier, during that time frame."

Each message has the date and time each call came in, after each one, we wait a few seconds, before playing the next. They go from begging me to hear him out, so I'm sorry she means nothing to me, to you will not divorce me, and finally, to if I can't have you, then no one will. He is seething with anger in every message.

Once they have all been played, I'm completely freaked the fuck out! I look at Morgan, thinking why couldn't I have found a decent normal man like this to fall in love with? I can admit now that I'm not as in love with him, as I once was. If I was a different person, then we might have made it work, but he and I are like oil and water. We will never be good for each other. I know I can't be with him anymore because he will destroy me. I will always care about him in a way because he gave me my beautiful children, but he is toxic to my life.

Leaving Morgan's office, I head to the rental property. I really like it, and it fits the kids and my needs very well. With all that's happening and how quickly, I just don't feel comfortable signing a long-term lease, right now. So instead, I decide to wait.

"Ava, this is a beautiful property, and thank you for showing it to me. At this time, I need to speak with my kids. Can I get back to you?"

"Absolutely, and please, take all the time you need. Just call me once you have made your decision."

"Thank you so much, Ava."

Maybe this is the start of a new beginning.

Claire

I lay with Molly on her bed, looking at houses for rent just in case. I don't know if I want to stay here or not. It's going to be hard constantly seeing Colton and Clarissa together, so I need to check out all my options. After looking for a while, I finally see a house that takes my breath away. It's the one I've always dreamt about. Sitting straight up, I grab the laptop to stare at the pictures, falling even more in love with the inside.

It's a two-story white, farm house with black shutters and a black steel roof. The lawn is full of rich green grass and flower beds around the porch, which wrap around the entire house. It's beautiful, and it really needs to be mine. I start searching for the address, but I stop, seeing a big problem. *It's in Colorado.*

"Why does the house being in Colorado have to be a problem? Can't you just move?" Molly asks.

"Are you trying to kick me out already? If us staying here is too much, please let me know, and we can crash at a hotel or something." She moved us in with her, until I can find a new place.

"No! You guys are fine here. I'm just thinking maybe you need a change of scenery. What better way to start your new beginning than with a final goodbye to this place?"

"I was actually thinking the same thing, but I need to talk to the kids, before I do anything. Maybe, after they graduate, then we can move."

"Mom, Carson and I both graduate soon. We have nothing holding us here, so let's go check the house out, and then we can go from there. Spring break is next week, and it's the perfect reason for us to go," Carly says, standing in the doorway.

"What about Carson? Do you think he wants to move?"

"I have nothing holding me here either, so let's blow this place. I'm done with all the drama around here. You told us how dad was cheating, but we already knew of some of it. This is for us, as much as it is for you. We are so tired of not knowing, which one of our friend's moms our dad might have banged. We are also tired of looking at younger kids, wondering if they could be our siblings. We need a new beginning, and in order to get that, we have to start with a goodbye to the past." Carson says, speaking up behind Carly.

"Okay, then. It looks like I'll be booking a trip to Colorado." I start to look up airfares, but they stop me.

"No, Mom. How about the three of us drive?"

"Okay, so it's a road trip with my kids." I say, sounding excited, and everyone laughs.

51

It Begins with Goodbye

******

Twenty-one hours later, we finally make it there, and the house is perfect. It's even prettier in person. It's so peaceful here, and the flowers are so vibrant and colorful. "I could sit on the porch and swing for days."

"Wow, Mom. Listen to you already, and this is just the outside," Carly chuckles at me. Oops, I guess my thoughts came out of my mouth.

"You have no idea. It's the house straight out of my dreams."

"Well, let's not waste any more time." I jump out of the car and start walking up the sidewalk, as my phone rings. I sigh with relief, when I see it's Molly, and not Colton.

"Hey Molly. What's up?"

"Claire, where are you?" Her tone sounds terrified and low.

"Why?" I ask, trying not to freak out.

"It's Colton. He says he needs you."

"What do you mean he needs me?" I walk away from the kids, so they can't hear this conversation.

"Shit, I don't know. He called me with some excuse about you being in an accident, and that you were asking for me, so Frank and I raced over here. When we got here, he told us that you were mad and wouldn't talk to him, so he wanted me to call you. I was about to lay into him, when his phone rang, and he went outside to answer the call. What do you want us to do here?"

"Listen to me carefully, you and Frank need to leave there now. I'm going to meet with the real estate agent here and get this process moving." I'm pacing and panicking because I don't want anything to happen to my friends. She agrees to leave, and as soon as I hang up with her, I'm on the phone with my attorney.

"Morgan, the kids and I are in Colorado, checking out a new potential house, and Colton called my friend, Molly. He told her some story about me being in an accident, and when she got to the house, he said he needed them to get me to talk to him." He tells me not to worry about it, and that he'll handle things on his end, and I hang up feeling a lot better.

Walking into the house, I feel a calm wash over me, as I realize this is where I'm meant to be. I'm smiling from ear to ear, as I follow behind Mrs. Paige, the real estate agent, as we go from room to room. The kitchen is my absolute favorite. It's yellow with black appliances and grey cupboards, and it's just stunning.

"If you don't like the color, you can change it. There is also a half bathroom right here under the stairs." She says, as I notice the dining room is pale blue, and it's large enough for a table. There is an incredible view of the woods and running stream behind the house, and the living room is large with a fireplace. I stand here, picturing myself decorating for Christmas, and my stomach fills with butterflies.

All the bedrooms are upstairs, so we walk up slowly. The first one is large enough for a king size bed and dresser, leaving plenty of room to move around. The next door is a bathroom, and it's a peach color with cream around the top of the walls.

Walking down the hallway, I realize the opposite side is the next bedroom, and it's just as large as the first one, and the only difference is this one is an indigo blue color. The next door is a linen closet, and then, at the complete end of the hall, is the master bedroom, which is light grey. It honestly feels like such a peaceful room. I'm so comfortable in here, like I've been here forever. This room has an attached bathroom with a claw foot bathtub too. *It's even more beautiful than I ever imagined.*

Mrs. Paige tells me about the skylights in every bedroom and both of the full bathrooms, and I didn't even notice them. "So, do you like it?" She asks me with a smile, while holding the application in her hands.

"No, I don't just like it. I'm in love with it, and I would move in today, if I could. What do you guys think?" I ask the kids.

"I'll leave you to discuss this in private. I'll be downstairs, if you have any other questions, or anything else for me."

"Mom, it's beautiful. We should head back, pack up, and move in as soon as possible." Carly tells me, laying her head on my shoulder.

"I would love too, but I have to wait, until the divorce is final."

"Well, let's go talk to Mrs. Paige and see what our options are." She says, as we all head down stairs.

"Mrs. Paige, we would love nothing more than to start the paperwork today. However, I have to stay in Michigan, until my divorce is final. What are our options?"

"We can start the paperwork, and if you're approved by the bank, then you will officially be a homeowner in Colorado. More than likely, you will have to come down and sign papers once everything is done." She stops for a minute, as her whole face lights up. "I almost forgot the most important part. Come with me." I follow her, as she shows me the very high-tech security system.

"Let's sign some papers!"

I'm so excited, and I can feel the butterflies, even more so now. I can't wait to show everyone our new home. Carson was right. We need to make a clean break from Michigan and leave behind all the bad memories.

This is going to be amazing.

Claire

Once we get back home, the first place we go is to Morgan's office. He is on the phone, so we wait patiently for him to be done. Once he hangs up, he tells me that his brother, who is a police officer, has offered to go with us to the house. This really surprises me, but also gives me hope that I'm making the right choice.

I take a minute to call Molly, letting her know what is going on. I also ask, if she and Frank can help us move. "Oh babe, I'm so excited. I knew that house was for you just by seeing your face, when you saw it."

"Hey, are you and Frank busy tonight? Can I borrow you both to help Carly, Carson, and I move our stuff out and into a storage unit?"

Molly squeals with excitement and hollers, "Are you kidding me? Of course, we will help you pack and move. Hang on, I'm going to jump on the bed and wake Frank up!"

I can literally hear her running through the house, throwing open the door, and jumping on the bed. "They are finally leaving the good for nothing bastard spawn of Satan, and we get to help her pack, so they can start the process of moving into their new home. Now, get up lazy!"

I hear Frank in the background saying, "Molly, you know I love you, right?"

"Well, duh. Everyone does, silly boy."

"Well, get out, so I can get in the shower and get ready to move our girl!"

I laugh, as I hear her happy squeals, but it also makes me sad, knowing that they have worried over me for so long. My face must show my worry, like I'm about to cry, because Morgan looks panicked, as he watches. Everyone has always told me that I don't have a poker face.

Morgan says, "Hey, no need to feel sad. They love you and will always worry, if you're in the perfect relationship or not. It's human nature just like you worry about them, Carly, Carson, and everyone else."

I hear sniffles, coming through the line. "Oh, shit. Molly, you okay, babe?"

"Yeah, and that was a very honest statement. Some people only care about what is important to them, but you have always been a caring person. I'm just excited that you are getting a new and fresh start. Anyway, we will meet you there in about thirty minutes. Sound good?"

"Yeah, babe. I just want you to know that I love you and will always care about you." Wrapping my arms around my babies, as they walk in, I breathe in their unique scent. Carson smells of spice mixed with earth, and Carly smells of vanilla and cinnamon.

I close my eyes and pray this goes easy, so we can move on with our lives. "Okay, guys. Let's do this." I turn, introducing everyone. "Carson and Carly, this is Morgan. Morgan, this is my son Carson, and my daughter Carly. Morgan's brother is on the police department, and he's going to meet us at the house, so we can pack and move our stuff. We were also approved for the house in Colorado."

"Oh, baby. I love a man in uniform!" Leave it to Carly to break the ice, as everyone starts laughing.

"Now, let's go get our stuff, and then start our happily ever." We get in our cars and drive, heading to the house. When we get there, I sigh, when I see that not only is Colton's truck here, but Clarissa's small car is too.

"Well Morgan, you're about to see my crazy life, before your eyes, so brace yourself." I say to him, as we get out of the car and walk to the front door. He starts to say something, but I already have my mask in place. Morgan quickly introduces me to his brother, Ben, and the uniformed officer, Pete. If Morgan wouldn't have said Ben was his brother, I wouldn't have known. They look completely different. Where Morgan has dark hair and chocolate eyes, Ben has blond hair and blue eyes. He's kinda like a typical surfer in the 50s. Pete looks like the boy next door with his hair all over, like he just brushed his hands through it.

Walking over to Molly and Frank, who are standing with the kids, I introduce everyone. I notice Molly checking out Morgan, and if I wasn't so distracted, then I'd meddle in setting them up.

"Okay, guys. Let's go in and get started." I walk up and look at the officer. "Should I knock, or just go in?" Before he can answer, the door swings open, and there stands Colton.

"Well, look at what I found. What is it that I can do for you?"

"Colton, please don't make this harder than it needs to be. Just let the kids and I get our stuff, and we will be out of here. Then, you can do what you want."

"What makes you think you're going to take my kids from me?" He is seething through his teeth.

The officer steps in and says, "Sir, the kids are old enough to decide, where they want to stay. If either of them wants to stay with you, then they can. Now, we can get a judge involved, or we can act like adults here. I'll talk to them each separately and find out what they want to do."

"She's already filled their head with lies about me, but you go ahead and talk to them."

"Nonetheless, I have to make sure this is what the kids want. Can you and your companion please step outside with my partner, while I speak with the children?"

"Yeah, I guess, but I don't want her taking anything that belongs to Clarissa or me."

"Sir, I can promise she will not take anything that doesn't belong to her."

I walk in the house with Morgan, Molly, and Frank right behind me, as Carson and Carly walk towards me, looking like someone just hit their pet. "Mom, why do we have to talk to the police without you?" I open my mouth to say something, but Morgan stops me.

"This is standard procedure, and the officers will ask you some questions. Just answer them honestly, and also know that whatever you say, won't hurt your mom or dad. Okay? Now, you two will be separated, so no one is influencing anyone, but when the officer is speaking with you, I'll be right there."

The kids try to look around Morgan to me, but he blocks their way. As their mother, it's killing me that I can't be there to protect them. "Okay, let's head to the bedroom and start getting my clothes and stuff ready." We walk into the room I once shared with my husband. I look at the bed I once thought was special, because it was ours, and now, I know it meant nothing to him. I was just a warm body, and something he used for his entertainment.

On the bed is my favorite blanket with a huge wet spot, and I know it's just him being spiteful and mean. My necklace is also there, and I have been wanting it. It's the infinity symbol with my birthstone on one side, and Colton's on the other. Apparently, he has jokes today. Well, I don't have time for this. I need to be the responsible parent for our kids.

I walk to the linen closet, grabbing my suitcases, and start dropping my clothes into them from the dresser, as Molly tries to fold them and make them nice. No, fuck that. I just need to get my shit and get out, before I end up in jail tonight. Once my dresser drawers are empty, I go back into my closet, grabbing my clothes, throwing the hangers on the floor, and filling the suitcases with as much as I can fit. I reach down, grabbing the handles and taking my clothes downstairs by the handfuls, and then placing them in the backseat of my car.

It Begins with Goodbye

Colton stands there holding Clarissa, smirking at me the whole time. I walk by, acting as if I don't have a care in the world, as he joked about earlier, and now, the joke is on him. Walking up to Morgan, I glance back at Colton, and then quickly turn back. I remember seeing all the fishing pictures in his office, so it gives me an idea.

"Hey, you like to hunt and fish, right?" He shakes his head up and down, and I continue, "Well, here is a paid trip for you and Ben to Alaska, as a thank you for everything you have done for me." I notice Colton's face turning red, as his mouth drops open.

"You should shut your mouth, so you don't catch a fly." I throw Colton a quick wink, turning and walking back to the house to finish bringing my clothes out. Damn, that felt good.

I'm in the zone, when I hear something, so I look over to Colton, standing next to me in the bedroom. He must have slipped in the back of the house. "Babe, can we talk this out. I want you and the kids in my life. I'm so sorry for everything." He begs.

"Will you please just stop for a minute and look at our marriage? It has been up and down over the years, but it's over. For the past fifteen years, I realize I haven't been living, and I've been just a shell of a person. I'm not happy, and I don't trust you, so no, we can't talk or work this out. We. Are. Done."

As he walks away, I hear him mumbling about a gift that he gave to Clarissa. I know right then that this is all about the trip. He doesn't care about me one single bit. He still thinks he has control over me with his sweet words, but he has another thing coming.

Turning I say, "You know, if I truly believed you loved her, I would feel sorry for her. Well, maybe. However, you both will get sick of each other, or you will cheat on her just like you did me. The only innocent person involved in this mess is the life you created together, but I will not be a part of that. You two made your choice, and now, you must live with it. You can't blame anyone except yourselves. I pray to God that you don't fuck up this kid. The only people I care about are the two that came from our marriage. At least, that's the only good thing about all those years. And right now, they're packing all of their stuff, so we can start our second happily ever after without you. You're right, though. I'm not sad or sorry because I know I gave this my all. You didn't, and that's on you."

"That's our biggest problem, Claire. You never showed any emotion. If you would have shown a tenth of that emotion from that last statement, I would have fought harder. We could still have our happily ever after, but I was never enough for you."

"Do you even believe that bullshit? You are the one who couldn't keep his dick in his pants ever. Maybe you have some insecurity issues, but that's on you. I was the one who felt like I was never enough, but I don't have to explain myself to you anymore. I can't, no that's not right, I won't bow down. You're not better than me, and I deserve better than what I've been given for the last fifteen years."

Turning to go back inside my bedroom, I find more memories and little things that I thought meant so much to us and our lives. Now, I know they meant nothing, and that pisses me off again. How could I feel have felt so much for someone, who felt absolutely nothing for me? *Where did I go wrong? Is there something wrong with me?* This is the shit that keeps running through my head. Vaguely, I hear Molly on the phone, saying she thinks I'm having a nervous breakdown.

Well, what am I supposed to be having? I mean, come on. First, it was my husband, and then my fucking twin sister. The person who is literally supposed to be my other half. *Who does that shit?* Fuck, I need to get my shit together, before Carly and Carson see me. "Guys, can you finish my clothes? I'm going to get my stuff from the bathroom."

"We love you, and of course, we are here for you, so please don't lock the door." Molly says, and I walk over, wrapping my arms around my best friend.

"I promise I'm not, Molly. I just need a minute or two. I know it will hurt less in time, but right now, I need the pain." I walk into the bathroom, pulling up my Spotify app, and hitting play on one of my favorite songs *"Wanted You More"* by Lady Antebellum.

Yes, this song is so me right now.

Grabbing my body and hair care products, I allow a few tears to flow, because I feel as though I'm losing a part of my identity. I've always been Colton's wife, and Carly and Carson's Mom. Yes, I'm also a nurse and a damn good friend, but this hurts more than I thought. I know I will eventually heal and grow from this, and it will take some time, but someday, I'll get there. I look around, realizing just how little of me is in this house. Is this why I'm so easy to replace? No, the right person won't want to replace me.

I will be enough!

I know I still have Molly and Frank, and they won't leave me. They love me, and I them, and I

70

couldn't have done this without them. I own that shit, but I won't hold them back, because I care about them too much. They know how hard this is for all of us. I mean, they are busting their asses to help get us out of here, as quickly as possible.

I grab some bags and walk down the hall, seeing Carly crying on her bed. "Frank, can you get these?" He grabs the bags, as I walk into her room. She stares up at me with tear stained cheeks and snot coming out of her nose, so I walk up, wrapping her in my arms. "Baby girl, what's wrong? Tell Momma, so I can fix it for you."

"Is Dad really having a baby with Aunt Clarissa? Why did he do this to us? Am I a bad kid, or does he hate me? Is this some type of punishment?" She hits me with so many questions.

"Carly Lynn, I don't ever want to hear you say something like that again. Let me get your brother in here, so I can answer any questions you both may have. Hopefully, I can help you both, as much as I can. Carson Phillip, come in here please!"

"You rang. Oh, shit. What's wrong, Carly? Did he hit you?" He asks, looking at me.

"No, now sit down here and listen to me. Yes, your dad is having a baby with Aunt Clarissa, and we know how. The most important thing is this," I make sure that both of them are paying attention to me, stressing the next few words. "This has absolutely nothing to do with either of you. It's not some form of punishment, and neither your father nor I hate you. You are both amazing kids, and we love you very much. This is about your dad and me. Sometimes, forever doesn't quite work out. Life is a gamble, and if you never try, then you'll never truly live. I don't regret anything that has happened between your father and me, even the hard stuff has taught me a lesson, making me the person I am today. I need you guys to always remember, no matter what happens in life, you two are always the most important people, and everything I do is with you guys in mind."

We all wrap our arms around each other, and I hear Colton clearing his throat from the doorway. "Maybe I should've been here for this conversation, since it involves me."

"Really? Don't you think you've done enough?" Carson snaps out.

"Carson, please just listen. I'm not going to make excuses or try and sugar coat what I've done. Was it wrong? Yes, but should I really be disowned by my family?"

"Colton, you may want to rethink asking these questions, right now." I say softly, yet firmly.

"Dad, you cheated more than once, and yes, Carly and I have always known." Carson states as matter of fact, and it breaks my heart. I thought I was protecting them by staying and not saying anything.

"There is a lot that happened in our marriage that you don't know about, and we both have made mistakes. Your mom is completely right, and we both love you two more than anything in the world. Our divorce is not because of you. We just grew apart,

73

and honestly, we should've done this a long time ago. However, we're not punishing anyone, ourselves included."

"Thank you, Colton. I truly hope you find what you're looking for, and the happiness that I could never give you." He nods his head, presses a kiss to both kids' heads, and whispers, "I'm sorry." As he turns and leaves.

I sit there with my kids holding them, while they let all the hurt and anger out. I don't know how long we sit there wrapped together, until Carson sits up and wipes his eyes, as he informs us that he's starving. We all laugh, as the tension begins to break.

He turns, looking to both Carly and I, as he says, "I love you both, but I think we have cried enough over him, so as soon as we leave here, there will be no more tears. It's truly time to start our second happily ever after."

"You are absolutely right, and I love you so much. Thank you. Carly, you good with that?"

"Yes, but I need some moose tracks tonight."

"I'm good with that. Carson, what can I get you?"

"Pizza from our favorite pizza place with pepperoni and bacon."

"Okay, I'll order it, when I get the cars loaded, so let's roll."

About that time, Morgan walks into the room, "Everything is loaded, except what you guys want in your cars." He says, and we all thank him.

Walking through the entire house once more, is bittersweet because this was supposed to be our forever home. It makes me sad, as I think back to all the memories I'm leaving here. *Bringing the kids home from the hospital, decorating the nursery, their first steps, their first words, and their first everything really.*

Molly wraps her arms around me, as she whispers, "At least, you get to take the memories with you in your heart, and he can't keep them from you."

"Thank you. Now, let's go, so I can feed everyone."

Laughing the guys say, "Finally." As I walk out the door for the final time, I wonder where Colton went, but in this moment, I know that I don't really care.

"He took Clarissa out of here, after he helped load up the SUVs with everything from downstairs he wanted you to have, including all of the pots, pans, and dishes. He asked me to give you this letter, but you're not to read it, until after everyone leaves tonight, and the kids go to bed." Frank tells me softly. Almost as if he's afraid of hurting my heart any more.

"Thanks, Frank. You're the best friend a girl could ever have, and I love you so much."

"Doll, you only love me cause I'm gay. Plus, I have such great taste in men and clothes."

"Oh, ha ha. You caught me. Now, Molly and I can check out guys with you!"

"Sure, you can, sweetheart. By the way, I think she has the hots for your lawyer. She needs a good guy because the last one was hard on her."

"Shit, I didn't even know she was seeing someone. I'm such a shitty friend."

"No doll, you have been dealing with your own stuff. She understands and loves you, so don't worry, because she will dish, when she's ready."

"You're so right. You can't get her to talk, until she's ready."

"Yep, that's our girl!" "Let's roll, doll."

Morgan leads the way with Carly, Carson, and Ben, following close behind. The police officer stays back with me, as I stop at the end of the driveway and silently say goodbye one last time, allowing a few tears to flow freely. After a while, I begin the drive to my new temporary home with the kids.

The more I drive the more my mind spins with all of this mess. I've tried to see this from Colton's point of view, but I can't. I've told him, since day one, that if he wanted out to please be honest about it. Yes, it would've hurt, but I wouldn't have hated him. Honestly, I still don't know if I actually hate him. I hate the situation that's a given. I'm more disappointed in my sister than anything. Clarissa knew how much it hurt me, when he cheated, and how I felt about myself, yet she still did it. I almost want to know why, but then I question is it truly worth knowing? I don't know, and only time will be able to tell.

I pull into my new driveway, and it hits me all of a sudden that I'm alone. I'm the one responsible for all the decisions made and for every mistake that might occur. It's all one hundred percent on me.

God, is this really my life now?

I start recognizing that I'm about to have a panic attack. The air isn't coming, and my heart feels as if it's about to beat right out of my chest. My palms are so clammy, and my whole-body shakes. The nausea is almost too much to bear, and I open my door, as I put my head between my knees, trying to even out my breathing. Some people think it's so easy to breathe evenly, but they have no idea. After a while, I start feeling in better control of myself, as I open my eyes, seeing Morgan standing in the garage, watching me.

"Sorry I took so long."

"Please don't be sorry. Molly ordered the pizza, and I'm going to run and get it, so I'll be back. I just want you to understand one thing. You are not in this alone. I know we haven't known each other long, but I'm here, if you need me. So please, let me be your friend."

"Okay, thank you very much. That means a lot. Oh yeah, here is my debit card for the pizza." I say, handing him my card.

"Sure, I'll take your card, but Molly and I have it covered, and she asked to ride with me. Ben and his partner, Brett, are off duty now, and they are inside with Carson, playing Call of Duty on the Xbox 360. I think they're long lost brothers. Frank has a date, so he had to get beautified, and Carly went with him. She said she'd be back, so I hope it's okay that I told her to go ahead and go."

"Yeah, she needs some time alone to deal with stuff her own way. As soon as I can get it through her head that it's not her fault, I'm hoping things will be better. Thanks again, and I'll see you and Molly in a bit. Oh Morgan, I've seen the way Molly looks at you. My advice, for what it's worth, is to take a chance. Life is too short to let something good slip away." As I walk away, I feel his eyes on me, and I know he is thinking hard about what I said. I hope our friendship continues to grow into more with time. He seems like a wonderful person.

Waiting for everyone to come back, I decide to unpack my bedroom and put everything away. I take a quick shower, throw on my yoga pants and a t-shirt, brush my hair and teeth, and then put my hair into a messy knot on my head. I walk into Carson's room and start making his bed, as they play the Xbox.

"Hey Mom. You want to play?" "You're a funny guy, Carson."

"What's so funny? Brett's wife plays with him all the time, and she's damn good." Ben says, looking right at me.

"I didn't know you were married, Brett. How long, and what's her name?" He gets a dreamy look on his face, as his smile lights up the room.

"Her name is Bailey Jane, and we just celebrated eight years together, and no, we don't have any kids. We knew, before marriage, that we couldn't have any children, but I get her, so no worries. She'll like you, Molly, and Frank. The next time you guys do your girls night let me know, and I'll send her over."

"Sounds great. Is she busy tonight? She's more than welcome."

"Nah, she is going to school right now, but thanks anyway. Actually, I think I'm going to head on home, so I can help her study."

"Have a great night and thank you so much for everything. Carson, when the girls have their ladies' night, hit me up, and I'll try to get off, so we can play again."

"What about you, Ben? Do you have a lady?"

"I don't think there is just one that can handle me." We laugh, but then he gets serious. "There is someone, and we've been talking and hanging out. I want more, but she is hesitant."

"Should we be worried?"

"Oh, hell no. It's nothing like that. Her dad was pretty mean, when she was younger, and he actually ended up killing her mom. Strike one against me is because I have a penis. Strike two is that I'm a cop, and he was one also, which is how he got away with all the abuse. However, he did go to prison for rape, but he didn't last two months, after his sentencing. For now, we're just talking and taking it slow. I must admit, at first, I thought Morgan had the hots for you, but now, I see it's Molly. Believe me though, if Janelle didn't already own my heart, I'd be all over you."

"Dude, that's my mom, and don't ever think of her like that. It's the bro code."

"I hate to be the one to tell you, but everyone, including your friends, thinks your mom is hot. Hell, even Frank does, and he's gay."

"Okay, guys. Let's change the topic. I need to work on me and my problems, before I even think of getting into a relationship." I walk out, heading to Carly's room to make up her bed. After I finish a few more things, I go downstairs, putting some stuff away, but I feel the exhaustion wash over me. Slowly I climb the stairs, and as I pass by Carson's room, I tell him I'm going to bed.

"You can't go to bed. You haven't eaten, yet."

"I love you, but right now, I need to sleep for a while. I worked a twelve-hour shift Friday and only slept like three hours, before I had to get up and meet Morgan. I really just need to sleep. I promise, I'll be okay."

I slowly walk down the hallway to my room, leaving the door open, as I sit down on the bed. *I really did it.* I left my husband, and then cut all ties with my sister. Gosh, what happened to my life? I never wanted any of this to happen. I just want to be happy.

I will be happy, and I don't *need* a man. I have myself and my kids. I'm going to call Dr. Savage tomorrow and talk these feelings out. I know this doesn't make me weak for talking to someone. I just need to vent more than anything. Then, she and I can review them, so I can get on the path of healing. As I plug my phone in to charge, I see I have some messages. There are twelve in all, and most are from Clarissa.

Clarissa: You ruined my life.

Clarissa: You destroyed Colton. He's drunk at the bar because of you.

Clarissa: You should be thanking me for making him happy.

And it goes on and on, but I just leave them, because I know I will need them for my case. I send Molly and Carly a text, letting them know I'm going to bed. I lean over, making sure my Nook is plugged in, and then shut the lights off. I lay in the darkness for a few minutes, before sleep finally takes over.

Claire

I toss and turn all night long, thinking about the decisions that are weighing heavy on my mind and heart. Am I doing the right thing? Am I setting myself up for failure? Will things ever get better?

With a heavy heart, I grab my phone, heading downstairs to make a phone call. I need a place, where I can be alone, in order get some expert advice. I go outside to the pool house, closing the door and letting out a sigh, as I make my way over to the lounge.

With shaking hands, I place a call to Dr. Savage on her private line. It rings twice, before she answers. "I wondered how long it would take, before you'd call me."

"You know doc, as funny as you are, I think you could make at least double your money, as a comedian. If I were you, I would seriously think of a career change."

"Well, then who would you call for expert advice?"

"I still have your cell number, so I can call you anytime."

"Ha ha. You're a funny girl this morning. Okay, now that we've gotten that out of our systems. How about you tell me the real reason you're calling me at 6:45 on this lovely Sunday morning?"

I start at the beginning, telling her everything. When I get to the part where he said we both made mistakes, I begin really unloading.

"I so was pissed off. I mean, how fucking dare he talk about me like that. He's the one that cheated not just once, but several times. And this time, it's with my motherfucking twin sister. I just held it in and told the kids I loved them. I'm completely heartbroken because the kids and I moved. I'm the one leaving the house they were raised in. I mean, he betrayed our trust and vows, so why should we have to leave the only home we have had for so many years? Molly was there, and she reminded me that the house may no longer be mine, but the memories always will be." With tears rolling down my face, I can finally admit out loud, "I know she's right." I take a long, deep breath, before I continue.

"I know we are toxic for each other, but it still hurts, even though it has been over for a long time. I always thought we had forever, and I guess we did, until I made the decision that I've had enough. Is this supposed to hurt? Am I supposed to feel guilt, hatred, and anger? I know they are all honest emotions, and not everyone feels the same way. I also know there is no right or wrong answer, when it comes to feelings. I guess I just need to hear that I did everything I could, but right now, I'm not even sure that will help. I know I need to let go, but how am I supposed to move on?" I say, sitting in my chair and drawing lines on a scrap piece of paper. I don't know what it is about doodling, but it helps me get everything out.

"Maybe I'm stupid, but how can he just let go of the vows and promises we made? I have so much hurt and anger built up towards him for being a coward and cheating. Am I that much of a horrible person that he couldn't just come and tell me? And let's not forget the anger and hatred towards Clarissa." With angry tears streaming down my face, I wait for the doctor to tell me what I need to hear.

"Listen Claire, you know you are not the only one to blame. This was a relationship, which means, if you both don't put forth the effort, then it's not going to work. He wanted something that he didn't need to work for, and women made that easy for him. You're right, if he loved you as he promised to, then he wouldn't need another woman. Sure, he could've been attracted to them, but he wouldn't have acted on it. You are entitled to your feelings, whatever they may be. He hurt you deeply, and this is not something you can simply just *get over*. Your heart, mind, body, and soul need time to heal and adjust." Dr. Savage calmly tells me, as she pauses for a minute.

"You cannot control how your children feel. All you can do is make sure they know how much you love and care about them. You can't reassure them that he loves them because he must do that. His relationship with the kids has no bearing on you, and he has to choose how's it's going to play out. I know you want to make everything perfect for them, but the real world isn't perfect, and they will adjust because they are awesome kids." She stops again for a minute, letting me take all of this in.

"Molly was right. The memories will always be with you in your heart and mind, and there's nothing he can do to stop those. I don't think you guys were toxic for each other. However, once he made the decision to be unfaithful and emotionally abusive towards you, he became toxic for you. I believe with everything in me that, if you hadn't already been in here seeing me and holding your ground, you wouldn't have gotten your degree or be where you are today. You are one hundred percent right. There is no right or wrong answer, when dealing with feelings. You can feel any way you choose to do so, and I nor anyone else can tell you how to feel, or if it's right or wrong. You're going to feel hurt, anger, and maybe hatred to an extent, because he betrayed your trust and lied to you several times." I know what she is saying is true, and this is exactly what I need.

"The reason you can't just let it go is because you care, and the relationship ended in a way that has hurt you. Yes, he cheated, and you have given in time and time again, but this time, it was deliberate. Both of them knew that being together would hurt you more than anything. They used your feelings against you. I'm very surprised you aren't more upset at Clarissa, because she knew all of your feelings, and what you have already been through."

"I'm plenty pissed at her. I'm just trying to get all my anger out one person at a time."

"Claire, I want you to write a letter to both Clarissa and Colton. You may or may not give them the letters, but this will help you let go of some of the anger towards them. I think this will help you."

"Okay, I can do that. When can I see you, so that you can read the letters?"

"Can you have them done Tuesday? I will be here between four and five. Just remember, they are just for you and no one else. We can talk about how you're feeling, and what the next step will be."

"Yes, that works for me. See ya at 4:00 on Tuesday. Thanks for always listening."

Walking over to the window, after I finish my call, I decide to take a swim in the pool. Going to get my suit, I turn some music on, and then stop by Carson's door, when I hear him up moving around. I give a quick knock, as he yells, "Come on in."

He looks up, seeing me, "Hey Momma. What's up?"

"Nothing babe. Aren't you and your dad going fishing today?"

"Yeah, but I feel like he cheated on all of us, so I'm not going."

I let out a sigh, knowing this is going to suck ass. "Listen, he is still your dad, and I want you to have a relationship with him. You guys need that. I also want that for Carly, so please just think about going and spending time with him. Don't shut your relationship off with him over a part of our relationship ending. You and your sister only have a little longer, and then you're going to be off to college and starting your lives. Spend time with your dad, while he is here. People don't live forever. I wish with everything inside me that I could have my dad back, and only if he were as healthy as he was, when I was a kid. Just promise to keep an open mind. I'm not saying move in with him, but don't cut him completely out of your life."

"Okay, Mom. I will do this for you. If he says one bad thing though, I make no promises."

"Thank you. This makes me happy. I love you, Carson."

"Love you too, Momma."

Walking down to my room, my phone starts to ring. Looking down, I see my soon to be ex's name. *Oh my God, what does Colton want now?*

"Hello."

"Hey. What are you up to this morning?" He sounds so chipper and happy.

"Why are you calling me?"

"Can't I just call my wife?" He says, like he is begging me with his voice to believe it.

"Listen, we're getting a divorce. I can't do this anymore, and I shouldn't have to."

"Okay, you're right. I wanted to know if you would be willing to do a baby shower for Clarissa and me? It would mean so much to us. Also, we would like you to be our child's godmother." I stop walking and put my hand to the wall. I must have heard him wrong. He has lost his flipping mind.

"Are you fucking serious? Wait, are you drunk? You have to be because you cannot seriously think that I'm going to do anything for you guys. No, I will not do a baby show or be your child's godmother. I can't just act like this didn't happen. Please don't ask Carson or Carly either. And Colton, don't call me anymore with stupid bullshit."

Forgetting all about swimming, I decide to do the exercise that Dr. Savage suggested this morning. Grabbing paper and pen, I sit down and write my letter to Colton.

Dear Colton,

As much as I don't want to do this, I'm writing a letter, so I can express how I'm feeling. Some of it may not be nice, but it needs to be said. Why did you have to be a coward? Why couldn't you just come to me? I would have

let you go, if that's what you truly wanted. What is worse
is that you cheated with my sister. Who does that?

I'm so sorry that I couldn't be who and what you
needed. Please believe me, when I say, I truly tried and
wanted to be your everything. I think I figured out where
our problems started. In the very beginning, you wanted
me to not go back to work and just stay home, and I
couldn't. That's not me. That was strike one. Strike two
was that you treated me like I was just there to please you.
Strike three was the way you treated me because I put the
kids before you. Maybe that's a good mom trait, and maybe
it's not, but I did the best for them. We had a great run,
and you gave me two amazing children. For that, I can't be
sorry.

In the end, it seems there was no room for just me
in your heart. Still, I tried so hard to change your mind. I
want you to be a part of the kids' lives always. With that
being said, I cannot be a part of your life. My heart has
always been yours, and I will always care about you for no
other reason than Carson and Carly. You have taught me
so much about myself. Thank you for allowing me to be a
mother and a wife. You know the old saying, you are

stronger than you think. It's one hundred percent right. Last year, I would have probably forgiven you and taken you back. Now, I'm strong enough to let you go.

I truly hope you find happiness and love in your life. I can't say I'm sorry it's not with me because I'm worth so much more that. Someday, I will find real love, but right now, I'm focusing on me. I believe that when you find the one, you shouldn't have to change, or try to be enough. You simply will be, and I want that for me.

So, this is me letting you go. I will talk to you about Carson and Carly only. Please don't call and ask me for anything else because the answer is no.

I need time for my heart to heal. I've come to realize that I should have left you a long time ago, after you betrayed me the first time. Again, I'm stronger than I was, but I still have a long way to go. I never want to see you unhappy, even though you wrecked me. I also hope you would want the same for me. I'm still so broken right now, but I know in time, I will be ready to give love another chance.

It Begins with Goodbye

I need for you to do some things for me. If you see me at the store, on the street, at our children's sporting events, then please leave me alone. Just pretend I'm not there. I need time. I need space, and I need you out of my life. I wish you nothing but the best, and maybe one day, we will be friends or at least civil.

All my best,

Claire

Claire

After reading over the letter, I feel better for getting it all down. The hurt is still there and will be for a while, but now, I know I will move on and be a better person.

I grab my swim suit, heading into my bathroom to change. Looking at myself in the mirror, I can definitely see changes. Wow, I've lost a lot of weight, since I wore this last. I grab a t-shirt, sliding it over my suit, as I grab my Nook and phone. I make my way downstairs, heading out to the pool in my backyard. I hook my phone up to the speakers, slip my shirt off, and then walk to the edge of the pool and dive in.

Man, this water feels incredible on my skin. Swimming around in the pool feels so refreshing. I'm relaxed fully for the first time in years. After I do about fifteen laps, I start feeling it in my legs, so I switch over, floating on my back. *I could really get used to this.*

Seeing a shadow on the water, I look to the side, seeing Morgan and Molly standing there watching me. "Guys, I'm not suicidal."

"What are you talking about, chick? We never said that."

"Don't bullshit a bull-shitter. You guys were watching to make sure I'm safe. I will admit to being angry, but he sure as hell isn't getting that kind of control on my life. I will be okay, I promise."

"Well, you won't mind if I join you, then?"

"No, Molly. I think I have another suit in my dresser upstairs."

I watch in total shock, as my best friend takes her clothes off, in front of my lawyer, and dives in. "Molly, what the fuck?"

"What? I'm just living a little."

"My lawyer is literally standing right there."

"Christ, Claire. He has seen everything I have before, I'm sure. You should join in. You're fucking beautiful, and I wish I had your body."

"Thank you. That makes me feel good. Well, I still don't want to be naked in front of him. Plus, I barely know him. I love you, but you're crazy."

"Well, good bitch, because I'm not going anywhere, and I love you, too."

Getting out to get some sun, I look over to Morgan, "Hey. If you want to swim, I can go get a pair of Carson's trunks."

"Would you please?"

"Yep. Be right back!"

It Begins with Goodbye

As I start to make my way upstairs, I swear I hear Morgan say, "You're going to pay for that later, my dear." Maybe they will find a happily ever after together. I get the swimming trunks, while also getting Molly a swimming suit. I don't need Carson coming down to the pool, seeing my friend swimming in the nude.

Heading back down, I stop and grab three bottles of water out of the fridge. When I walk out, Morgan is on the phone in what looks like a heated conversation. Wonder what that is all about? I see Molly, laying on the lounge chair, so I walk over, handing her the suit, as she smiles back, but it doesn't quite reach her eyes.

"What's wrong, little lady?" She just looks over at Morgan and back at me.

"Come on. Give it time, babe. You guys just met a couple days ago, and it wasn't the best way either. I see the way he looks at you. He's definitely interested." She shakes her head, but before she can say anything, Morgan walks over.

"Hey Morgan. Is everything, okay? You looked kinda stressed on the phone over there."

"No, but I won't l lie or hide this from you. Colton and Carson were in a fight, and Carson broke his nose. Clarissa is pushing for Colton to press charges."

"Oh, my God. That stupid, bitch. I just want one peaceful day. Let me change, so I can go get my boy."

I run upstairs, taking two steps at a time and try to hurry, so I can get to Carson. I throw on a tank top and shorts, and then I grab extra money, because I don't know if there will be bail money or not. I wonder what happened to cause Carson to go off like that. He's always had a slight temper, but usually, he can control it. So, someone had to provoke him. It doesn't matter though because he's my son, and my only priority right now. Running back down the stairs, I say, "Let's roll if you're going."

Molly says, "Hell yeah, I'm going. I want to see Colton bleeding like a stuck pig! And I can't wait to give Carson a high five. He's a badass kid." Looking at Morgan, she states, "He gets his badass ways from his Aunt Molly, ya know."

We all burst out laughing. As we make our way to the car, I have a feeling this is going to end up being a long ass day. Hopefully, I won't end up in jail with my son.

******

We finally make it to the hospital, but we are stopped by a hysterical Clarissa. "That's the bastard's mom. I want her to go to jail, if Colton won't press charges on Carson, just because he's his son. He certainly didn't care, when he broke his dad's nose and eye socket."

"Look Clarissa, I know you're worried about Colton, but you need to stop calling my son names. If the police need to take me in, then fine I'll go, but don't think you're better than either of us. These are our children, and it's probably for the best, if you remember that. Now, please tell me where my son is, so we can get the fuck out of here."

"Fine, follow me, but be quiet because Colton is resting. Today has been very stressful for both of us. Not only did his son break his nose, but I had to be checked out due to cramping." Her voice is like nails on a chalkboard, and I roll my eyes.

As we walk down the hallway, I hear Carson, "You were not having any cramping. You just wanted to be checked out because you weren't the center of attention. Dad, I still don't see what you see in that broad. Guess we'll have to hang out, when she's gone, because I won't be going to your house, if she's there."

"I need you to respect her, as I plan on marrying her. She is also carrying your half-sibling."

"You can spew that shit about half-siblings all day long, but I'm telling you straight up, Carly is the only sibling I have or will ever have. I'm not asking you to choose us over her or the spawn, but don't expect us to be over the moon. I mean, you destroyed our family. You have always told me to be honest about everything, and you do the complete opposite. I feel like our whole lives have been a lie."

"What do you want from me? What can I do to make this better or easier for you and your sister?" Colton asks, sounding a bit annoyed.

"I don't know how else to say it, but you can't do anything. The damage is already done. You had our trust and respect, and then you threw it back in our faces. It's going to take time to earn it back, but I can't promise that you will ever get it. You really hurt us, Dad. I know if I was with a chick then I would never be with her sister. That would be like mom dating Uncle Zander." Carson says, reminding me of Colton's brother, and how much I have hated him from the beginning.

"That will never happen. We have problems being in the same room. How are you?" I say, stepping into the room.

"Hey Momma. I'm okay. How are you?"

"Really Carson?" I know I sound pissy, but I cannot believe this happened. In what universe is it okay, to allow a woman to threaten your child? "How am I? Well, let me tell you. My lawyer gets a call that you've been in a fight with your dad, and I need to come and get you, because Clarissa is pushing to press charges. So, I drop everything to rush over here. So, I'm not doing too good at the moment."

"Mom, you don't need to worry. Dad isn't going to let anyone press charges. Thank you for rushing to get me though. I love you."

"I love you, too. It's my job, as your mom, to worry and to come get you, when you're in trouble. Sometimes, when you're in love or lust, you do and say things you wouldn't normally say. I had no way of knowing for sure or not if your dad would or wouldn't press charges, just because Clarissa asked him to." Just then, Molly and Morgan walk through the doors.

"There is my badass nephew! Dude, I told Morgan you get your badass genes from me." She turns, looking at Colton, "I hope your face hurts cause it's killing me."

"Okay Molly, how about you and Morgan take your nephew and get a drink or something, so I can have a second with Colton." "Why do I miss all the good stuff?"

"Carson, go with Molly now and wait for me in the waiting room, and remember, best behavior, please."

They walk away, as Carson says, "I hate when she uses the mom voice. Good thing it didn't happen to you and Carly, or your credit cards would be on fire from your retail therapy."

"Oh, look Morgan, we have our own comedian with us." They all laugh, as they disappear around the corner.

I wait a bit, before looking at Colton. "Well, what happened?"

"Don't worry about it, babe. We are guys, and we had a difference of opinion, but now, we are good."

"I'm not your babe, and I most certainly will be worrying about it, when your little lap dog is trying to get either my son or myself thrown in jail. Last time I checked, a difference in opinion didn't lead to a broken nose and eye socket. So, one more time, what happened?"

"I asked if Clarissa could go fishing with us, but he wanted to spend time with just me. She is very clingy, and she wants to do everything with me. She started talking about our honeymoon, and then asked if we could do a family one, after the one for just us. That also pissed Carson off. She then asked him, if he and Carly would host a baby shower, and if they would be the baby's godparents. She told him that we had asked you, but you had refused."

I can actually feel my blood pressure rising, and there's no telling how red my face is. "Jesus fucking Christ, Colton! What the actual fuck were you thinking? Seriously, you cannot be this stupid! You break up our family, because you fuck up and get my sister pregnant, and then tell Carson he still needs to have a relationship with you and your girlfriend. Why would you think it was a good idea to take her? And a honeymoon? You're not even divorced, and you're talking about getting married already. Wow, I'm glad to know my level of importance now. You're such a cock sucker, and I seriously despise you." I stop for a minute, trying to catch my breath, before I continue.

"No, you can't take my kids on your fucking honeymoon. The reason Clarissa is so clingy is because you cheated with her, so she knows you will have no problem cheating on her. I told you no for the baby shower for all of us, and the same goes for being the spawn's godparents. Use the fucking head on your shoulders for one second. If I cheated and got pregnant, would you want to be the godparent for that child? Would you want that thrown in your face at every turn? I don't and neither do the kids, so for the love of God, fucking stop. Look, I think it will be best to wait a couple weeks, before you contact the kids or me again. We all need to get our emotions under control, because right now, every time I see you or her, I want to rip your dick off and shove it down your throat sideways. If you have any questions, then call my lawyer." I turn not giving him time to say a fucking word.

When I walk out, Clarissa starts running her mouth, and I tell her three times to shut it. She isn't letting up, and she even pokes her nasty finger in my chest. "Stupid, bitch. I can say what I want."

I'm done letting her talk to me like that, so I get close to her face, letting her have it. "How did my pussy taste, after you sucked it off his cock? I'm sure you've had my sloppy seconds plenty of times now. Think about this even though you guys have been fucking for a year and a half, if I wanted him, he'd still be with me. No, you didn't win, I did. I deserve so much more, not only from my husband, but more importantly from the person I shared a womb with.

You can forget about me and my kids because we are done with the two of you." I turn to walk away, and she grabs my arm. I try jerking it away, but she has a tight grip. We struggle back and forth, and my hand finally slips free, but not before it connects with her nose, and blood starts spraying everywhere. Shit, this is not good. She is pregnant and will probably have my ass thrown in jail, even though it was an accident.

"I didn't mean to hit you, Clarissa. Are you okay?"

"Get away from me, you psycho." She turns, running back towards the room, leaving me to realize that my hand is starting to throb.

"Shit," I mutter, as I walk to the waiting room, holding my hand. Carson sees me first, and he jumps up, running to me. "Momma, what did you do? Is your hand broke? You have to get it checked out."

"Thank you, Dr. Carson. I'm a nurse I know it's probably broken or fractured, but I'm not staying here. I'll go to a different hospital to get it checked. I think I might have broken her nose, too. This is not good." I explain to everyone what happened between Clarissa and I in the hall.

"I'm not worried about her nose. We need to focus on your hand."

"Well, can you drive me to my hospital, so we can get this checked out, please? Oh, and grab my phone out of my purse, so you can call your sister."

"You know I love you more than anything, but I'm not touching your purse. I'm sorry, it just feels wrong to do so."

"Molly, please get my phone, so Carson can call his sister." Instead, he ignores both of us, as he uses his phone to call.

"Hey Carly. Mom wanted me to let you know we are at the hospital. Dad and I had an altercation, and I broke his nose and eye socket. I'll tell ya later all about it, but right now, I'm taking Mom into her hospital, because she thinks she might have broken her hand. Clarissa grabbed her arm, saying a bunch of horrible stuff, and Mom kept asking her to let her go. Anyways, long story short Mom jerked, and ended up breaking Clarissa's nose and possibly her own hand."

"Carson, I hate to cut your commentary short, but my hand is throbbing, so can we move this along? Just tell Carly to meet us at the hospital, please."

"Let's roll. You want me to still drive, or sit in the back with you?"

"Please drive, and Molly can sit with me. I need some meds. God, this hurts so bad."

"Morgan, do you think she will press charges against me?"

Looking over, I see Morgan and Molly, staring into each other's eyes. He never takes his eyes off of her, as he says, "She won't because you can press them on her, so it's best to just drop it. We need to get your hand checked out. Come on, babe." He says, grabbing Molly's hand and walking out the door.

"Well Carson, I guess I'll be sitting up front with you."

When we get to the car, as predicted, Molly and Morgan are in the back seat, as I get in the front. "Let's go get Rocky checked out!"

"Wow Molly, not only did he get your badassness, but he also got your smartassness, too. It's a hell of a combo. Do you think we can hold the jokes though, until I get some pain meds?"

"Sorry, Momma."

"It's okay. Let's just go. Your sister is probably there waiting for us."

We finally make it to the hospital, and Carly is there already. "Oh, Mom. Are you okay? What am I going to do with you? Carson, how could you let this happen?"

"Can you please hold off on yelling at me. I'm really starting to hurt now. Oh, and your brother has something to tell you. Good luck, Carson. I'm going to see, if they can see me."

Molly

I watch, as Carly stands there looking so much like Claire, waiting for Carson to tell her the story.

"What do you need to tell me? Did something else happen today?" He begins telling her everything that has happened, since him and Colton went fishing.

"Oh my God, Carson. You could have gone to jail. What were you thinking?"

"I know, but he pushed me, and then he kept pushing, saying things like she is going to be our mom. I don't fucking think so, and that spawn they are having is not our sibling. It's just us, sis. You, me,

116

and Mom. I know you and Mom worry, but I couldn't stop myself. I love you and will try to be better, I promise."

"I love you, too, and I'm sorry this is just so hard for me. I feel like this is all my fault for some reason, like I've let everyone in the family down. What did I do wrong for Dad to hate us?"

"Carly Lynn, come with me to the lady's room. Carson, you go with Morgan and check on your mom."

We walk arm in arm the entire way, and I open the door, looking under every stall door, making sure we are alone. Once I'm satisfied, we walk back to the door, and she leans her back against it, as I stare into her eyes.

"What makes you so sure that your mom and dad splitting is your fault? Shouldn't it be their fault? What if they weren't meant to be together?"

"I just can't wrap my head around the fact that someone, who is always supposed to be there and love me, Carson, and Mom, can just walk away so easily. It's like we don't mean anything to him. That's what hurts me the most."

"Your dad made his choices, and I know it hurts, but you're not taking the blame for this. You had to have known that they weren't happy for a while now. You're a smart girl Carly, but you need to let this go. I know your mom talked to Dr. Savage, and she is making her face her demons head on. It may take her a while, but she is at least getting her feelings out. I also think that would help you as well. Maybe grab a journal and write out how you are feeling about everything lately. Please just know, I'm always here, and I'm on your side. I just need you to jump. Don't be afraid because I'll catch you."

"Oh, Molly. I love you so much, and I will get a journal, as soon as we get Momma home. Once I'm done, will you read over it for me? I don't really believe it's my fault, but it just hurts to know I'm so easily replaceable. I know it has to be much worse on Momma. Ugh, I have probably made it hard on her, too. Damn, why do I always have to cause more problems?"

"You don't cause problems, and your mom is fine. She already knows how you feel, and how you work through problems. Just like she knows how Carson, Frank, and I do. Yes, I will read over whatever you decide to write, if you want me to. Come on, let's go see your mom."

We leave the bathroom, walking down the hall, when Carly's phone chirps with a text. I watch her, as her smile is one of true happiness. "Everything okay, kiddo?"

"Yes, but I can't wait to tell you about Xavier. He is so awesome," she looks at her phone again, frowning before looking back up at me. "Dad and Clarissa are here to check on Mom."

I let out a sigh, as Carly looks back at her phone, typing quickly. "I just asked Xavier to come here. I need a friend right now. This is a lot of drama, and I just need someone to lean on."

"I'm so proud of you, and I can't wait to meet him. I'm not excited about how this is going to go

119

down, so let's go make sure your brother doesn't do anything stupid."

We both laugh, as we walk towards Claire's room. We hear people talking, so I take a deep breath and square my shoulders, as we walk in together. Claire is sitting in the chair with her nook. I swear that thing is connected to her. The sky could crash down around her, and she wouldn't even notice. Carson is laying on the bed, playing on his phone, as Colton and Clarissa stand there looking between the two of them.

"Claire, has the doctor been in, yet?" I ask with my voice full of concern.

"Yeah, but I'll tell you about it, after dumb and dumber leave. They have no right being here, much less knowing any more of my business."

"You are still my goddamn wife, and I deserve to know."

"What language do you actually speak? I have stated it several times in English now, and you still don't get it. We are over and done, so move on. I may legally still be your wife, but you don't deserve to know anything about me. You lost that right, when you cheated, and I was dumb enough to give you another chance, but you kept on doing it. Who knows how many times you cheated, when I didn't find out. Then on our anniversary, I find out you are fucking my twin sister, and she's pregnant with your baby. How does it feel Clarissa listening to him call me his wife still, if you guys are so in love? You don't like, huh? Well me either, so once again, I'm done with you. Get the fuck out!"

Holy shit!

Claire's badass side just came out, and she just looks back down at her tablet, like nothing happened. I look over at Carson, and he has a huge smile on his face.

Carly walks in a minute later, "Hey Mom. You want anything from the cafeteria? Oh hey, Dad. I didn't know you were here, and look, you brought it with you. I was hoping you had come to your senses and wanted our family back. Guess that's just wishful thinking on my part."

"Yes, Carly. It's wishful thinking because your daddy has a real woman now, and we are going to be a family. All five of us."

I'm completely shocked that Colton just let Clarissa talk to Carly that way. She has always been a daddy's girl. Looking at her face, I can see the devastation written all over it. I'm praying so hard that this doesn't cause her to start having trust issues with men.

"Clarissa, I don't know what kinda drugs you're on, but they can't be good for the baby. Carson and I will never be your family. I honestly feel sorry for the spawn. I also almost feel sorry for my dad, but he made his choice, so he has to live with it. Besides, you will never be half the woman my mom is."

"Carly, my girl. Come see me. I missed you today, baby girl. Where were you this morning, when your brother and I had our argument?"

"Are you seriously asking me that? To think, I thought I was special, and that you loved me. I had a track meet that you were supposed to be at with my brother."

"Don't be so dramatic. Your dad has a new family now, so he can't come to your silly meets." Clarissa chimes in.

"Wow Dad, I didn't realize your voice had changed so much. Maybe, you should check and see, if you have a vagina also. Clarissa just so you know my dad ran track, which is why I do it. It's our thing, like fishing is with Carson. It's fine I don't need him to come to anything else of mine ever again. I hope you both get what you deserve."

We all turn, when there is a knock on the door. It slightly opens, revealing a nice-looking young boy. No wonder Carly was so giddy earlier.

"Hey Carly. You okay, sweet girl?" He walks right over to her, like nobody else is in the room, wrapping his arms around her. My heart sighs at how adorable they are together.

Carson finally speaks up, "Hey Xavier. What are you doing here, man?"

"Your sister needed a friend, so I came. So, don't get all big brother on me now. I told you man-to-man that I like your sister, and I'm going for it."

"Yeah you did, but I still don't have to like it."

"You can both put your penises away. I'm right here, and I can make decisions on my own. What is it with guys who think a woman can't make a simple decision without their input? First, the one man I thought would never betray and hurt me this deep does, so thanks for that, Dad." She glares at him, as she continues, "Now, I have my brother acting like I have to get permission to date, or hell, even be friends with someone." She turns, looking at Xavier, "If you think I need you..."

He puts his finger over her lips, stopping the words. "Babe, I don't think you need me, but I hope you do. When I have a good or bad day, I need to tell you. Sometimes, when I'm just sitting around the house, I need to hear your voice or to see you. So, do I think you need me? No, but I need you." He leans down, brushing his lips over hers, as he grabs her hand, intertwining their fingers. "Let's go talk."

Looking at Claire, I say, "Wow, I have never seen Carly or Carson like that."

"Listen Molly, Xavier used to be a major player, and then one day I was waiting for Carly to finish her track practice. I was sitting on the bleachers, and he came and sat with me and asked, which chick I was waiting for. I pointed Carly out, telling him she was my sister. He hasn't had a girl anywhere around him since, and he has been trying to get Carly to go out with him. He has been to every track meet, he stays over for her practices, brings her favorite Gatorade, or whatever she wants. I tried to keep them away from each other, but they are like magnets and metal. If this goes south, I'm going to feel responsible."

Before I can speak up, Claire starts in, "I cannot believe you would say something like that.

Your sister is intelligent, and I'm sure she knows what kind of man he is. You know I'm afraid I have made a mistake. Please listen to me. I'm not angry that I lost so much time with your dad, and I need you to remember this now and always. If you don't try, you're not living. If you don't love and lose, you're not trying. I need you to try and to live. If you never have a heart break, you have never really loved, and I want more than anything for you to love. I know it hurts, but I'd rather love and hurt, than to not love at all. Your sister is going to be okay. Maybe it will work out and be forever, but then again, maybe not. At least, she is trying, and that's all anyone can ask."

I couldn't have said it better myself.

Claire

After a while, the doctor steps in. "Hey Dr. Frazier. Long time no see."

"Hello Claire. I see you brought a lot of friends with you this evening."

"No, I didn't. I brought my kids, and my friends Morgan and Molly. However, that asshole and whore over there seem to think that they deserve to know my business, even though I've asked them to leave multiple times." I can feel the pain meds kicking in because I have no filter.

"Okay,   well I kindly need you two to please leave, so we can get this bay opened back up."

Colton finally speaks for the first time, since Carly and Xavier left. "Fine, but Carson please call or text me, and let me know what's wrong with your mom. I guess I'm going to stop and see Carly and that boy on my way out of here."

Carson looks furious. "Fuck no you're not, and neither am I. Mom's hand is probably broken because of your bitch there, and you need to leave Carly alone."

Colton looks almost heart broken. "I will need to know for insurance reasons, son."

"Colton quit grasping at straws. I have my own insurance and haven't been on your policy, since I started working," I state.

"Well, Carly is my daughter, and I have every right to see her." Just then, her and Xavier walk in still holding hands, and she looks happy and at peace.

"I don't want to see you, Dad. You have hurt me so bad, and I'm sorry if this hurts you, but right now, I need some time for me. I can't worry about you. I would feel differently, if you ever thought of Carson, Mom, or me, instead of yourself. But you didn't, and you don't. Actually, you've only ever thought of yourself, so that's what we are going to do."

I want to jump up and wrap Carly up in my arms. I'm so proud of her for standing up to her dad like that. Shaking his head, Colton walks out with Clarissa running behind him to catch up.

Dr. Frazier waits a minute, before speaking, "Well Claire, you have broken your hand, and I'm also taking you off work for at least two weeks. Any special color you want the cast?"

"Nope, let's just do this." Finally leaving the hospital with an orange cast and a new blue sharpie, we are head to the pharmacy to get my meds. Hopefully, my hand heals quickly.

It Begins with Goodbye

******

Two days later, I'm sitting here just hanging out with the kids. It's been nice just spending some quality time with them. I've been thinking seriously about getting them a dog. They have both been begging for one for a while, so why not, yeah?

"Okay, guys. I've been thinking about something. As long as both of you help me out, I'm thinking of getting a dog. So, what do you guys think? You want a dog?" Both scream yes loudly at the same time, making me giggle.

We all get dressed, and then head to the local animal shelter. Carson sees a German Shepard, and it's love at first sight for both of them. Meanwhile, Carly finds a black cat with a couple of white patches on its belly, and again, it's love at first sight. I guess we are getting a dog and a cat today.

We are all Detroit Tiger fans, so when we leave, we have Verlander the German Shepherd and

Miggy the cat. Both of my children are happy, so I'm happy. I will do anything for them.

Claire

A year and a half later.

Today is the day my kids graduate from high school, and I'm so proud of both of them. They both decided to go to Colorado to school, and Xavier is also going to be with Carly. I haven't spoken to Colton or Clarissa, since we signed the divorce papers. I texted Colton to let him know about the graduation time and the party afterwards, but he didn't respond, so I have no idea if they are coming. I planned a party for the kids right after, and I didn't even ask if he was doing something. I just invited him and his family to ours.

Carson has been over to see him a couple times, but he always has a time limit, unless Clarissa is there. Carly still refuses to see him. He called and told her to come to the hospital cause her sister was here, but she didn't go. They also named her Caitlynn after Carly, and it pissed her off even more. That weekend we all went and got matching tattoos of hearts with angel wings on the side. I added the kid's initials on the top of the wings in mine, Carson got mine and Carly's initials, and she has mine and Carson's initials.

Carly also took the school's track team to state, and they won. That's how she received a full scholarship to Colorado State, and the reason why Carson chose to go with her. Xavier is still waiting for his letter, but he's going, even if he doesn't get accepted. His family doesn't really approve, but that isn't stopping him. Honestly, I'm not sure he even wants to go to college. I think he just wants to be with Carly. Carson has also let up on being so

133

protective of Carly with Xavier. All three of them have a great relationship now.

"I hope they don't cause a bunch of trouble today." Someone says, snapping me back into the present. The ceremony went great, and now, we are all at the party.

I look over, seeing Colton and Clarissa, walking towards the kids. Morgan and Molly, who have officially become a couple, must have seen them also, because they move quicker, getting to the kids first. I really hope they don't start a bunch of drama today.

I put on a smile, and then walk towards the two people that hurt me, but they also helped me in a way I'm very grateful for. "Hey guys. Thanks for coming to support Carson and Carly. There is plenty of food and drinks, so make yourselves at home."

"Cut the shit, Claire. You knew we were having our kids party today. Why do you feel like you always have to one up us every time?"

"I'm sorry, Clarissa. I didn't realize they were your kids. I sent a message to Colton about the party, but I never got a response, so I figured you guys weren't doing anything. The kids didn't even know you were having one for them. I don't feel like me being a good parent is one-upping anyone. This is me doing my job! Now, if you'll excuse me, I need to visit with family that came for *my* kids. If you cannot act like civilized adults, then you need to leave. Today is about my kids and not about either of you. I mean, neither of you even bothered to show up to watch the actual graduation."

I know everyone thinks I let Clarissa get away with her part in everything, but the truth is she was pregnant. Now, if she keeps running her mouth, it's going to get ugly. I stay away from them for the rest of the party. I hear her several times, trying to tell people lies, but today isn't about anyone or anything, except Carson and Carly. As hard as it is, I keep my mouth shut. After everyone finally leaves, I start cleaning up. After picking up the kitchen, I head back outside, seeing Colton and Clarissa are still here, and my mom is playing with their offspring.

I yell inside to the kids, letting them know their dad is still here. They both come out, looking at him like he has four heads. "Why are you here? What I mean is why did you come at all? You didn't even come and see us graduate." Carly spits out.

Clarissa immediately starts running her mouth, "You ungrateful, little brats. He is still your dad, and we will both be treated with respect. He deserves to be here. After all, he paid for all of this." I've had enough. This is my kids party, and this conversation has absolutely nothing to do with her.

"Whoa, hold the fuck up! You don't get to call my kids ungrateful brats. They both have jobs and graduated with 4.0 GPAs. It's their party, and if they want you to leave, then you shouldn't be here. Colton hasn't given anyone of us a dime, since before I moved out. I don't know where you got your information, but you better get a better source. Now, I believe my kids asked you to leave."

"Listen, I only want to be a part of my kids' lives," Colton remarks.

"I sent you a text, inviting you to come for your children. I didn't ask you to bring your whore, so she could degrade the kids. Why do you want to be a part of their lives now? You haven't really even tried. Ya know, it doesn't matter. This is up to them; I won't stop it, but I'm not going to push it either." I turn, leaving them standing there. I know if I hadn't walked away, then I would've said or done something that I might've needed my lawyer for.

As I take down tables and fill garbage bags up, I feel Clarissa watching me. It's kind of creeping me out. I run inside, putting on yoga capris and a t-shirt to finish the clean-up. I grab my earbuds, put them in, and crank up my Spotify, as I finish up.

As I make my way back outside, I see mom still has the baby, Carly and Xavier are stacking chairs up, and Carson is talking with his dad. I don't see Clarissa, but I'm not actively looking for her either. I take three bags of garbage to the dumpster, and on my way back, I feel someone grab my hair and yank. Without a doubt, I know it's Clarissa. Stupid bitch, it's on. I turn around, punching her square in the face, as blood goes everywhere. I try to stop hitting her, but I just can't. This has been a long time coming, and it feels good to get it out.

I feel arms wrap around me, pulling me away from her, as she lays there crying. Carson has me in a tight hold, and I can't move, so I just start screaming, "What the fuck are you crying for, you stupid whore?"

Carson pulls my ear buds out, keeping his arms around me, while rocking me, trying to get me to calm down. Once I'm finally calm, he starts telling me that Clarissa and Colton are having problems, and that Colton wants me back.

I feel like I'm in the twilight zone, right now. *This shit doesn't happen in real life, does it?*

I look around, noticing Carly is now standing with us. So, I turn, facing both of my children, "Is he serious? Does he honestly think I'd take his dumb ass back, after all this?"

"Mom, I didn't know about it, until today. That's what we were talking about, when you came back outside."

"I don't think you should even think about giving him another chance. He will choose her and every other woman over all of us every single time. But Mom, if you want to be with him, I'll stand behind your decision."

"Carly, I'm not taking him back. Not now, or hell not ever. I can't even be friends with him. Too much has happened but thank you for letting me know you have my back." What I don't tell them is that this is Colton, trying to play mind games again. Too bad for him, I've grown a lot in the past year, and I don't believe a damn thing that comes out of his mouth.

"You know I've always got your back. I told him I thought he has lost his damn mind, but he had to let you know how he feels, or he would always regret it. He also said he wants you and him to raise Caitlynn, as your own."

"Ugh, no. He should have thought about this, before he cheated. I'm not going back to who I used to be. He doesn't love me, nor do I love him. He's just afraid to be alone. Sometimes, you need to be alone to find out how strong you truly are. So, everyone can stop wondering and worrying." I see mom picking Clarissa up and taking her to her car.

After a few minutes, Mom comes back over, wrapping her arms around me, as she whispers, "I love you, and I'm so proud of you, but you need to make Colton and the kids understand where you're coming from, but more importantly, where you're going."

"I love you, too, Mom. Thank you." Stepping back from her, I turn, addressing everyone at once. "Carson, Carly, and Colton, please go inside and wait for me at the kitchen table. It's time we get everything out and in the open." I take a few minutes, getting my thoughts straight and ready to go. I shake off the nervous energy and put my big girl panties on. As I go inside, I hear Carly, yelling at her dad. "Okay, guys. We're not yelling tonight. We are going to sit down like adults and talk this out." I let everyone get settled in, before I start.

"Colton, you need to understand that I will never go back to you. We are done forever. We can't fix our marriage, because there is no trust here, and I won't live like that anymore." He starts to say something, but I hold up my hand. "Please wait until I'm done, and I'll give you the same courtesy. You have no idea the hurt that you've caused me. You should have been honest with me and told me you wanted out, but you didn't. You chose to cheat not once not twice, but several times that I know of. I need you to know that I don't hate you. Yes, I'm hurt, disappointed, and disgusted with you, but I'm working on not feeling negatively towards you. Someday, I'll be there, but that day is not today. The truth is even when I didn't trust you, I still loved you, but not now. I have my pride and my kids." I turn to

Carson, staring into his eyes, so I know he's paying attention to me.

"Son, I love you to the depths of my soul, but you need to have a relationship with your dad. I know he hurt you and let you down, but he is still your dad. I wish I could have my dad back. That just isn't in the cards for me, so please save your relationship, before it's too late." I let out a sigh, because I know this is going to be hard. Carly has such a passion in her, and it can be a curse just as much, as it is a blessing.

"Carly, you have always been a daddy's girl, and I'm sorry he hurt you. I wish I could take all the pain away from you, but I can't. I need you to remember that this is only making you stronger. It's a lesson on how nobody is perfect, and it will also help you understand what not to accept in a relationship. You should never feel second best or inadequate towards anyone. You are so beautiful and deserve everything. I love you, baby girl." I look towards Colton, to see if he has anything to say, but he only hangs his head. I know this is hard for everyone, but it needed to be said. I tell everyone goodnight, and then head to my room.

Two hours later, the kids come into my room, and I can tell they both have been crying. I don't say anything because there is nothing to say. I simply open my arms for them, as they both climb on the bed with me, and we all lay quietly. Finally, Carson softly asks me, "Mom, what are you going to do, when we are gone?"

"I will be fine. I have work, and that's all I really need."

"That's not a life."

"I actually got a new job, so we can move to our new house. I only have until the end of June here, so that's plenty of time for us to get settled in. I know you guys will be at college a lot, but there is still plenty of time to make memories at the new house." I pause for a minute, letting them take it all in.

"Also, I wanted to keep this house in case we ever wanted to come back, so Morgan and Molly are going to live here. To our new beginning. I love you guys more than you will ever know."

I have conflicted feelings. On one hand, I'm so excited to have this new start, but I'm also going to miss everyone, and more importantly, knowing how the hospital works. We all need to unwind, after this long stressful day, so I make an appointment to get my hair done tomorrow. Afterwards, Carly, Molly, and I are going to do a girl's day and get Mani's and Pedi's done.

******

As I walk into the salon the next day, I hear Clarissa's voice, and it makes me stop and listen. "She has cut us both off completely from the kids, and she doesn't even see Caitlyn. My heart is broken. I just want my twin back, but she won't even listen to me, and if I try to call, she denies it. I just don't know what else to do. I mean, we didn't mean to fall in love. It was just supposed to be sex." *Is this bitch for real right now?*

Stepping around the corner, I decide to confront this drama queen. "You should have never had sex with my husband for one. Two, you lost me, when you got pregnant, while we were married. As for my kids, they are welcome to see you or their dad anytime. They are the ones who choose not to, so don't blame me for that. I would see Caitlyn, but then, I'd have to see you. I have no desire for you in my life, as I have told you several times, you're dead to me."

"Claire, wait I- I'm sorry, okay. I didn't mean to fall for him. I just wanted to be you."

"Well Clarissa, I guess you got your wish, but you lost your twin in the process. I hope it was worth it." I turn and cancel my appointment. I'm not staying here with her a minute longer.

"Claire, I just need my sister back. Colton and I are having problems, and I need someone to talk to."

I stop by the door, listening to her spout this nonsense.

"Listen, I'm not your person anymore. I could care less, if you and Colton, fell off the face of the earth. Let me make this clear for you one last time. I'm done with both of you."

I head outside and get in my car, realizing I feel nothing at all. With a smile on my face, I go to meet my daughter to get pampered. Both girls are already there, so I head inside to get started. Carly gets lavender on both her fingers and toes, and I get passionate pink. Molly goes crazy, getting some type of blood red. I try to question her about the relationship with Morgan, but she diverts the situation.

"When you are ready, I'm here, and I'll always by on your side."

"I know, babe, but I just have to figure this out. It looks so easy from the outside looking in, but it's super hard. I'm so scared to make the wrong decision. Hell, I'm scared to make the right decision. I mean, what if it's right for me and wrong for him or vice versa?"

"Just breath, Molly. What's going on in your head? Let's talk this out."

"No, I'm sorry, Claire. Today is about girls' day and getting pampered. It's not about my problems."

"It doesn't matter where we are or what we are doing, you are important. I'll let you have today, but we will be discussing this. I don't like to see you this way."

"I promise, we will. Okay, enough with the sad shit. Let's go eat, so we can go shopping," Molly has her fake face on. She knows I can see through it, and I wish she would just tell me know what's going on. Ugh, I hate when I can't help someone, but I know she will tell me, when she is ready and not a second before. Knowing I'm not going to get anything else out of her, I let it go for now.

It Begins with Goodbye

We get to Olive Garden and eat, and like always, I box up my leftovers for Carson. Once we are done, we go to the mall. Carly goes to the shoes, Molly goes to Victoria's Secret, and I go to the scrub store, getting fifteen new outfits. I mean, who doesn't love cute scrubs? I head to find Carly, and she has twelve pairs of shoes picked out. This girl loves her shoes. I decide to grab a pair of Adidas, while I'm here. I need good support for my feet.

Finally, we make our way to Victoria's Secret. Molly already has a changing room for me and Carly set up. I reject all of the things, before I even go in. "You get me boy shorts, or I'll get my own. I will not be working with anything up my ass! Carly, stop laughing. I'm serious."

"They match the bras, so I got you all matching sets." Molly informs me with a serious look on her face.

"I don't match my stuff. I just grab whatever I can reach and put it on. Jeez, you know this." I look up to the ceiling, muttering, "Why do I let her talk me into this shit?" This is not going to end well for one of us. "Molly, you know that I love you, so please, go get me the matching boy shorts, or I'll walk out with nothing!"

"Fine," She screams, letting out a frustrated sigh. I almost feel sorry for her, but she knows me better than anyone. "You know, someday you're going to find a man to wear matching undergarments for, and you're going to thank me for showing you this store."

"I'm not looking for a man. I have Miggy and Verlander, and they are enough." I hold my hand up, expressing that I'm done. "We are done having this conversation, right now." I turn, heading into the dressing room, and a few minutes later, a pile of boy shorts slide under the door. A few seconds later, Molly comes out under the door. I should be shocked, but this is Molly we are talking about.

"Claire, I love you, and I only want you as happy as you want me. I know Colton and Clarissa

149

really fucked with your head, but please promise you will at least try to be open to the possibility of a relationship in the future?"

"I don't know if I can live with that pain again, and I will not live a lie. I can't be with someone who I feel absolutely nothing for. If someone catches my eye, then I'll try, I promise. Will you promise me the same?"

"Yes, I promise."

"I promise, too." Carly says through the wall, making us all giggle.

"Oh good, because we were worried Xavier isn't the one."

"Oh, shut it. I just wanted to add my two cents in. I love you old ladies."

"Okay, now get out whore, so I can try these on, and then, we can get on with our day." I only try on three sets, and then I've had enough. They are all the same size, so I know they will fit. I go out and find Molly and Carly, grabbing their stuff, as I head to the checkout. I pay for everything, as they both bitch, but I just give them a look.

I head to Bath and Body Works, so I can get my stock of a thousand wishes body wash, lotion, body spray, and hand sanitizer. Carly and Molly both get what they need, and we finally leave the store. Now, we are going to get ice cream, and then go to the movies for the rest of our girls' night.

"You ladies will be on your own, as I have a hot date with a very hot guy, who is right there waiting for me." With a wink, Carly is gone.

"Man, I remember those days." As soon as the words leave my mouth, I see Morgan standing there too. Well, there goes girls' night. Looks like it's just me, myself, and I. "Molly looks like you have a hot date also, chick. Have fun, and please, do something I wouldn't do!" Carrying everyone's bags, I make my way to the car, get everything in, and head home.

Once I get there, I draw a hot bubble bath, put my Spotify on, and then grab my Nook. An hour later, I'm a bit pissed off, because I'm in the middle of

Chasing You by Kelly Elliott, and my battery is getting low, and my water is getting cold, so I guess it's time to get out. First things first, I go into my room and plug in my nook, head back to the bathroom to get dried off, and then put lotion on. Heading back to my room, I climb into bed and start reading. The main guy, Greyson, is so hot, and I feel so bad for what the girl, Megan, went through. If Claire, from the book, were my daughter, I'd beat her ass. I can't wait for the next book, Loving You.

I yawn, looking over to the clock. *Holy crap.* It's 3:37 a.m. I guess I better get some sleep. I need to get to packing later today.

Claire

Two weeks later

Finally, the day is here, and I get to start my new beginning. I can't wait to see what the future has in store for me. I'm leaving a couple days, before the kids. It's kind of like a vacation. Twenty-one long hours later, I finally pull into my new driveway, and I feel a sense of peace and calm settle over me, as I make my way inside. I notice all the furniture has been delivered and set up, so I go through the place, falling in love all over again. My favorite part is the patio outback with a built-in bookcase. It's so beautiful here, and I have a great feeling about this place.

A week later the kids get here, and we have a month, before I start work, and they go back to school. This is amazing, and I'm so glad we decided to move. However, I miss Molly, Frank, Morgan, and Ben. It hasn't been too awkward with Ben, after our night together. He has asked several times for a repeat, but I have denied every time, saying I'd rather just be friends. I haven't told him he called me Janelle, and I know she holds his heart.

I look down, seeing that he is calling me again, and I guess I need to face the music. I think I'm just going to be honest with him.

"Hey Ben. How are you?" We chat back and forth for a bit, before I say, "Listen, I think we need to talk about what happened that night."

"Yeah, I know I called you Janelle, and I'm so sorry for that."

"I'm sorry, too. It's also partly my fault, if I would've just talked to you. I'm not angry. I just know I can't be more than friends with you. I'm hoping, when everyone else comes down here, you will as well, and maybe even Janelle can come also."

"Sounds good, and I will have to see about Janelle. Shit, I've got to run. We just a gotta call. I'll talk to you soon. Later, love." Well, that went better than I thought.

******

The next two weeks go by fast, as we all settle in. We absolutely love it here. I also love the hospital I work at. I got called in to come back early, and I couldn't turn it down. Some days, I go into Springtown, which is the next town over, and work in their ER. A couple of the local doctors have asked me to join in their practices, but I like the fast pace of the ER and helping people, before anyone else gets to, and it's never the same.

It Begins with Goodbye

Carly is also working here part time in the laundry, and she loves it. The hours are flexible, and they work around her track and schooling. Carson and Xavier are working construction, which they love. Their company also works around school schedules. Everyone from back home is coming for a visit in two weeks. I'm so excited, but I'm also nervous, because my mom is coming. I haven't talked to her, since the kid's graduation party, when I beat the hell out of Clarissa.

I've met a few nice people, since I've been here, but none of them are like Molly. However, there is a doctor, over at Springtown, that's hot. He has shown interest several times now by asking me out. I want to say yes, but I'm afraid. He makes it a point to talk to me constantly, but with my history, I'm scared. Even though, he is tall and delicious, and I swear he is straight out of one of my books.

The next week flies by, and then my mom calls, "Hey honey. Is it okay, if I bring Caitlynn with me, when I come down?"

"Of course, you can. It's just Clarissa isn't invited. I moved away for a reason, and she isn't going to fuck with my life. Actually, you don't have to leave at all. You can just live here with the kids and me forever."

"Please don't start with that today. I said I'd think about it, and I will, I promise. Now, I gotta go, and I'll see you guys in a couple weeks. Tell my grandbabies that I love them and you."

I have mixed feelings about this. I mean, Clarissa wanted to be me, so why would she let her kid come here? I would never send my kids on vacation without me. Oh well, to each their own I guess.

The next day Mom calls me again, telling me to look at my email. She sent me a letter that Clarissa wrote, and I need to read it. As much as I don't want too, I guess I'm a bit curious to see what it says.

It Begins with Goodbye

Dear Mom,

It's hard to put into words what I'm about to say, but I'm going to try my best. I gave birth to a beautiful little girl that I don't want. I feel like I should want to keep her, love her, and protect her, but I don't feel any of those things. I have tried, and everyone said maybe the feelings would come later, but they haven't, and I want to live without the burden of a child. I know that this makes me sound like a selfish asshole, and maybe I am, but I'm trying to do the right thing here. I want to be able to buy what I want and not worry, if I have enough money for diapers. I want to be able to go and do as I please. I don't want to have to think, "Did I find someone to watch Caitlynn?"

You're a protector, survivor, and a hero. You would give someone the shirt off your back, if it would make them smile. I'm asking you to raise my daughter, as your own. I have all the paperwork, and I want her to be legally yours. I cannot come back in a few years and take her. Colton agrees with me for different reasons. When we started our affair, we didn't set out to hurt you or Claire.

If I hadn't gotten pregnant, then no one would have ever found out.

I can't say I'm sorry it happened because I'm not. However, I'm sorry it hurt Claire. You know the saying, "Once in a while, right in the middle of an ordinary life, love gives us a fairy tale?" Well, he is my fairytale, and I hope you and Claire can accept this and our relationship. I know we hurt a lot of people, and our beginning isn't a very good one, but it's ours nonetheless. Please take care of her and love her like you have loved Carly and Carson. That is all that Colton and I ask of you. We know we have no right to ask this or anything of you, but we feel that you are the best person and the only one we trust for this.

Love always,

Clarissa and Colton

As I sit here, with tears rolling down my face, my heart breaks, because I should have known what was going on with Clarissa. I can't believe that I shared a womb with her. We have always been complete opposites. I'm the quiet one, because I like to sit at home and read, but Clarissa? She is immature, selfish, and loud, and she just acts like she doesn't think first. So, the question I ask myself is what do I do? Do I tell mom to raise Caitlynn, or do I tell her that I'll do it? Will she do it, or will she just give her to someone else? Would she be doing this, if I was still there?

This was meant to happen. Yes, it's heartbreaking, but it's life, which helps us learn lessons. As I sit here with a thousand different things running through my mind, I decide that I'll help mom raise Caitlynn, as if she were my own, and the first thing I need to do is call and let her know the change in events, and then, I guess I'm going shopping. Oh, I also need my lawyer to look over the paperwork. I think I'll call Morgan, after I call Mom. I know I was upset in the beginning about them having a child, and I have distanced myself from her, but the thing is she's completely innocent. It's not her fault she was born into this mess, so it isn't my place to shove her aside.

When I talk to Mom, she is so happy that Caitlynn will be taken care of. She is also thankful that Caitlynn will still be in the family. She was worried about how I would react, after what they did to me, but she is just a child and deserves the best out of life. Morgan has all the paperwork done, and all mom and I have to do is sign the papers, and we will be good.

Finally, I call Carson and Carly. They both have rooms here, but Carly mostly lives with Xavier, and Carson is staying in the dorms. I invite them over for dinner, letting them read the letter from Clarissa, and then tell them my decision on helping raise Caitlynn with Mom. Carson thinks it's a prank and wants to make sure everything is legal. He's afraid that Colton or Clarissa are going to come back and try to take her. I assured him that Morgan has filed all the paperwork, and they will not be able to take her from us now or ever. Carly is baffled and excited to have Caitlynn here with us. However, she is also hurt that two people she believed in ended up hurting both of us for their own selfish desires. She also understands why we are doing this, and they both support us.

We spend the rest of the evening enjoying dinner and just catching up. Xavier comes over, and when Carly goes to the restroom, he asks for our permission to marry her. Carson and I both agree. He isn't going to do it tonight, but it will be soon. The ring is beautiful with a diamond oval. It also has a white diamond on each side, and it's in white gold. The rest of the week is spent getting ready for everyone to visit and working doubles.

Claire

It's been a long two weeks, but today is finally the day I get to see Molly, Frank, Morgan, Ben, and Pete. Mom is coming tomorrow with Caitlynn because she has an ear infection. I have the steaks ready, the potatoes on the grill, and the corn on the cob already started. When everyone gets here, I hug everyone, and we all have tears in our eyes. I've missed these people so much.

We sit around getting caught up on everyone. Pete and Frank have started dating. Of course, Molly and Morgan are still doing whatever they are doing. I don't think they have put a label on it. Ben brought Janelle, and she seems nice. However, she seems a little pissed at him for whatever reason. I'll be considering that later tonight. I take everyone to their rooms. Morgan and Molly are rooming, Pete and Frank are rooming, and now, we have Janelle, and she doesn't like the idea of sharing a room with Ben. I ask if she wants to share with me, and Ben states, "That's not necessary, unless you have room for me as well."

Well, okay then. I guess they will be in the room together. I'll definitely sleep with earbuds in tonight. I go back downstairs and finish dinner, while everyone unwinds from the long trip. After dinner, we sit around and talk. Carly is falling asleep on Xavier's lap, so he takes her home. Carson also decides to go home, and everyone else decides to head to bed. That's good with me because it's been a very long day.

I'm sitting in bed reading, when there is a knock on my door. "Come in."

Janelle walks in, closing the door behind her. "Is my door in jeopardy of being broken down by Ben?"

She starts laughing, "No, he was getting in the shower, when I told him I needed to talk to you alone. He asked to come with me, but here I am. So, I'm just going to get this out. I know you and Ben hooked up once, and I'm sorry for how that turned out." I stop her right there.

"We're all adults, and it's not uncommon for the person you are with to have been with other people. It happened, and Ben and I are better suited, as friends than lovers. I hope you and I can become friends as well."

"The guy I was seeing hit me across the face, because I wouldn't have sex with him and his friend in a dance club for everyone to see. When Ben saw what was going on, he took me away, and we haven't looked back."

"Oh, sweetie. Do you want to stay here longer? Is there anything I can do to help you in another way?"

"No, thank you. Well, maybe in a different way actually. Ben and I want to get married here, and we are thinking of moving here. I just needed you to know that I don't want any hard feelings between us."

"What happened between Ben and I was never anything serious. I was in a bad place and so was he. We helped each other out, but I knew from the start you held his heart, and it was never going to be mine, nor is mine his. Please, let me know if you need or want help looking for houses or planning the wedding." We hear footsteps coming down the hall. "Thank you. Maybe tomorrow," she says, before leaving to go back to her room.

The next day I get called into work for a regular eight-hour shift. When I get here, I see the hot doctor clocking in. *God, it should be illegal to look like that.* I swear to all that is holy he has to be at least six feet and five inches of pure muscle. I saw him with a scrub top on one day, and his tattoo goes from his wrist to the underside of his shirt. *Oh, what I would give to follow it with my tongue.* And his ass, oh yeah, my lady parts are dancing. He has deep green eyes and brown hair that looks like he just rolled out of bed. He also has a beautiful square jaw. Honestly, he is what dreams are made of.

"Oh, looks like we get to work together again today. Must be my lucky day," he comments with a smirk.

"Lucky for you, but me, not so much, because I'm supposed to be on vacation today." Just then, our pagers go off, and we both run down the hallway to our patient. The day is steady, and we don't have a lot of downtime. I've been here for several hours and haven't taken a break, and I'm just ready to be home.

It Begins with Goodbye

Someone grabs my arm, I look up, seeing that it's the hot doctor. "Come on, let's go. We have fifteen minutes."

I pull back, looking into his eyes, "Where are we going, and why do we only need fifteen minutes?"

He bends down, whispering in my ear, "Baby, when I get to be with you, we will need way more than fifteen hours, let alone fifteen minutes. I'm taking you for a quick break, before you collapse on me." My insides instantly heat, and my mind goes straight to both of us laying naked, as I trace my tongue along his tattoos.

We walk to the cafeteria together, and I grab a bottle of water and a pack of crackers out of my pocket. I sit down at a table, as he sits across from me with his own water and sandwich. The conversation flows easily between us, and the more we talk the more I realize how sweet he is. When he is done eating, he looks up at me. "So, can I have your number?" He states in in serious tone.

"Umm, why would you want it?"

"Because I'm interested, and we've been on our first date already, so I think I should get your number now."

"I think you need to have your head examined." I say, shaking my head, laughing at him.

"Claire, I'm going to be very blunt, but honest with you, right now. I really like you, and I've been trying to ask you out for weeks now. I want to get to know you. The real you on a personal level. I want to know what makes you happy, or what pissed you off so much that you packed up and moved across country. I want to watch you as you sleep, and also be there when you first wake up. I also want to see the look of pure bliss on your face, as I make you come over and over. So again, can I please have your number, so I can call you, since you're on vacation? I want nothing more than to set up a date with you please." I can feel the blush running up my neck.

"My phone has sat on the table this whole time. All you had to do was grab it, and then put your number there. It takes two seconds to call or send a text message to yourself. I'll be back. I need to use the restroom." I leave my phone on the table, allowing him to put his number in.

When I come back, he looks pissed. Great, what did I do now?

"Who are these people with you?"

"What are you talking about?"

"Who are in the people in this picture with you?" I look down at my phone screen, as a smile spreads across my lips.

"Oh, those are my children. This is my son, Carson, and my daughter, Carly. I'm not married, and I have been divorced for a little a while now. I found out on our anniversary that he had been fucking my twin sister. They actually have a baby together now, and her name is Caitlynn. Recently, they decided they didn't want to be parents anymore, so my mom is bringing my niece here for me to help raise. Is there anything else you'd like to know about me, Maddox?" I feel so embarrassed that I just blurted out my personal problems. Maybe I did it because I feel like he'll lose interest. Or maybe, he might want to get to know me more. *Hell, I don't know what I'm thinking right now.*

His eyes go soft. "I'd say I'm sorry that your ex is a douche, but I'm not, because now, I have the chance to be with you. I'm sorry about your situation, and I'm not sure if I could help raise a child, knowing how she came to be. You're stronger than a lot of people would be."

"Thanks, I guess. Anyway, this conversation has been interesting, but I need to go." I start to walk away, but he falls into step beside me.

"So, how about I take you out Friday night?"

"Listen Maddox, my friends are here for two weeks, and my mom will be here tomorrow. Then, I'm going to help my mother raise a small child. I really don't know if I'm going to have time to date. I'm sorry."

"I'm not giving up, and I think Friday will be perfect. You'll have people here that can watch Caitlynn. Come on, what do you say?"

"I'll see what I can do. That's the best I got for you."

He gives me a cocky smirk, "At least, it wasn't a no. I will win you over, sweetheart. Mark my words."

I finish my shift at the same time as Maddox, and he clocks out, waiting for me. After grabbing our stuff, he walks me to my car. "Don't forget to text me. Enjoy your vacation."

Damn. Why does this man put butterflies in my stomach?

Claire

I sit in my car, watching him walk away. Man, those scrub pants do wonders for his ass. Mom calls, bringing me out of my dream. She tells me that Caitlynn isn't any better. I decide I'm going to meet her halfway, so she doesn't have to drive the whole way alone. I tell her to meet me tomorrow at 9:00 a.m. at the Illinois-Iowa state line.

With a sigh, I head home, so I can eat, shower, and go to bed, so I can get up and meet Mom. Not exactly how I planned my vacation, but it is what it is. I call Carly, asking her to go with me, and she agrees.

When I get home, I notice someone has already ordered pizza, and it must have just been delivered, because it's still hot. I grab a slice, on my way to the shower, and then it's bed for me. As soon as I hit the bed, I hear my phone ping.

Maddox: What are you doing?

Me: Just showered. You?

Maddox: Yes, please. □

Me: Ha, ha, ha.

Maddox: So, can we go out Friday?

Me: Don't know yet. I have to drive to meet my mom tomorrow.

Maddox: Oh. Want some company?

Me: Nah. My daughter is going, but thanks anyway.

Maddox: Call me when you leave, and I'll talk to you and keep you company, if you're not ready for me to meet your mom.

**Me: Ha! You're something else. Okay, I
need to get some sleep.**

**Maddox: Dream of me because I will
definitely dream of you. ;)**

Me: Maybe. □

Before I fall asleep, I head downstairs, letting
everyone know what's going on, and that I'm leaving
early to go get Mom and Caitlyn. Carly decides that
she and Xavier are staying at my house, so she
doesn't have to get up so early, and Carson takes my
car and changes the oil and fills the gas tank for me.

It feels like I just went to bed, when my alarm
goes off. I have a small Detroit Tigers cooler that I put
some water in, then I send Carly a text, so I don't
wake Xavier up, letting her know we will be leaving
in fifteen minutes. When we finally leave, I take the
wheel first, and Carly goes to sleep in the passenger
seat. I turn Spotify on, so I don't get sleepy. I've been
driving for about three hours, when my phone rings,

and I look down, seeing that it's the hot doctor. "Hello!"

"Hey, it's Maddox. What time are you leaving this morning?"

"Well, I left about four thirty, so I've been driving for three hours. We are actually getting ready to pull into a gas station here in Nebraska for gas and a bathroom break. What are you up to this morning?"

With a heavy sigh, he says, "I asked you to call me, when you left."

I don't want to sound like a bitch because I'm trying to be compassionate. "Look, I didn't even want to wake my daughter up, but I knew my mom would need someone else to drive her car back to my house. I also knew you worked yesterday, so I figured you'd want to sleep in a bit."

"Then why wouldn't you let me go with you? I could have driven your mom's car."

176

"Again, I didn't want to bother anyone. Can we please not fight? I just want to get my mom and Caitlynn and go home."

"Okay, can I ask you one question? Will you please give me a chance? I'm not asking for marriage or for me to take you to bed. I'm just asking for a chance."

"Maddox, I want you to really think about this. I'm about to help parent a toddler, whose mom and dad have just decided they want nothing to do with her. I have two kids in college. I promise I'm not playing hard to get. I just want to make sure you know what you're getting into and what you're asking of me, before I let my heart get involved."

"I get it. It's going to be hard work, but anything worth having, is worth the fight and the struggles. It makes it real. If it comes easy, then it will leave just as easy. I'm only asking for a chance. From the moment I first saw you, I knew you were different. I have never met anyone like you before."

Carly says, "Mom, give the guy a chance for God's sake. You are young and beautiful. Don't use Caitlynn, as an excuse, because Carson or I will watch her."

"Okay, you got yourself a date Friday night, unless Caitlynn is still sick. I'll call you, when I get to my mom, and thanks for checking on me."

"Anytime, beautiful. Thanks for letting me in. If you get sleepy or lonely, you can call me. I'm off today."

After a few more hours, we finally get to Mom. She is kind of tired, as Caitlynn has been cranky. I decide to take Caitlynn with me, and Carly is driving Mom's car, and they are planning on stopping to sleep tonight, but I want to drive as much as possible. Caitlynn clings to me, and I know it's because she thinks I'm her mom, and well, I guess now I am. Damn you Clarissa and Colton. Why did you do this to this poor little girl? No matter what my feelings were before, I can never mistreat this sweet little girl.

We stop off at Walmart to stretch our legs, and I buy a DVD, so she can watch it. She also finds a baby doll that she loves, so I get it for her. When we finish, we walk over to Subway, grabbing a sub, and then we sit and eat. I give Caitlynn her medicine again, and she gets sleepy, so it's time for us to hit the road. She's out, as soon as I get her in the seat.

I drive for a while, before I get bored with my own company and the radio. While I debate with myself if I should call Maddox or not, my phone rings, and the decision is out of my hands.

"Hello."

"Hey. You didn't call, and I was worried."

"Sorry, Caitlynn hasn't wanted to let go of me, and we went to Walmart to stretch our legs. I ended up getting her a DVD to watch, and she found a baby doll she wanted. Then, we went to subway for lunch, and she got her meds and is now sleeping."

"Who is riding with you besides Caitlynn?"

"No one. Carly is driving mom, and they are planning on sight-seeing and spending some time together, but I want to get home."

"I could have gone with you, so you didn't have to drive alone. I can have a friend meet with you, and I can ride the rest of the way with you."

"That's sweet, but we will be okay. If I get tired, I promise to pull over and sleep, and I'll call, if I do that."

"Thanks, doll. I have to say that I'm excited about seeing you Friday, even if we just hang out at your house."

This makes me giggle. "Yes, it will be fun, and to be honest, I'm excited also. I want to be honest with you. I have only been with one person in the last few years, who wasn't my husband. My ex had two affairs that I knew about, before the one with Clarissa. The first one I felt like I had to give him one more chance for the kids. Yes, I was young, but oh so dumb. The second one I kicked him out for a while, and he finally came to see the kids. When he left, they all cried, so again, I felt like I had to give him another chance for them. We did counseling together as a couple, as a family, and as individuals. I gave it my all, and it almost destroyed me. I had so much hatred built up inside of me for both Colton and Clarissa, and then I read the letter from Clarissa. Now, I just don't know how I feel. Shit, I'm sorry. I didn't mean to unload on you like that."

"I'm glad I'm here to listen, and I'm learning a lot about you. I would love to finish this conversation in person. I also have a past that is not perfect either. My former wife committed suicide because I gave her an ultimatum. I was busting my ass at medical school, and I thought she was going to nursing school. I found out, when I came home from classes sick one day, that she only played nurse with any male on campus that wanted to play. After that, she started working at a sex toy store. When I found out, again I put my foot down. Then, I found out she was with a sex operator. I told her it was me and her, or her and everyone else. She couldn't handle being exclusive, so I told her I couldn't handle her lifestyle, when I wanted forever. I left the next morning, and I found out she killed herself two weeks later. I felt like I let her down and caused her to kill herself. I know that I didn't, and she wasn't stable, but I've been to counseling. It's just not the same though with knowing in your heart and in your mind, because they are two different things. I have never felt a connection towards another person since, until you walked into my ER. It was a horrible trauma case, and you didn't even bat an eyelash. You walked right over and started feeling for the bleed. After we found it and saved the guy, my heart hasn't beat the same since then. You have literally turned my world on its side."

"Wow, you know how to make a girl feel special. So, Friday I was thinking of doing a BBQ with all my friends and family. I go back to work next Monday, and they will be here for another week or so. Is that okay for our date? I mean, you could bring your family or friends, if you want."

"That would be awesome, except my parents live in Oregon. I don't want to spend time with my normal friends. I just want to spend time with you."

"Okay well, I'll let you go, so you can rest, before you go back to work, and I'll talk to you soon."

"Sounds good, but just remember I'm here for whatever you need me for."

"Thank you. Bye."

"Bye, sweetheart."

Caitlynn and I drive all day, and then make it home at eleven forty-five at night. I'm so ready for bed. Thankfully, everyone is out, so I take Caitlynn up to give her a bath and her medicine again, and then get her already for bed. I'm going to let her sleep with me tonight, and tomorrow, we will work on her sleeping in her own bed. Both of us pass out, as soon as our heads hit the pillow.

When I wake up, I look at the clock, and it reads one o'clock. *Holy crap!* I was more tired than I realized. I notice right away that Caitlynn isn't there.

I jump up and run towards my door, when I hear her laughing followed by Carson laughing. With a sigh and my hand to my racing heart, I go use the bathroom and get dressed for the day.

As I head downstairs, Carson spots me. "Hey Mom. We thought we'd let you sleep. I hope we didn't wake you up."

"Nope, you didn't. What time did she get up?"

"Oh, about a half an hour ago. I changed her diaper, and we have been playing here. I also gave her some Cheerios."

"Thank you, Carson. Good morning, baby girl. How are you?"

"My Carson play ponies wif me."

"Yes, he's a good big brother, isn't he? C'mon babe, we gotta get your medicine in you, so you can get all better. Carson, have you talked to Carly or Grandma today?"

"Yes, they are planning on being here later this evening. Caitlynn do you want to go to the park and play with me?"

"Yes! I love the park."

"You don't have to take her. We can hang here, until I go pick up my check."

"Mom, we're fine. She's my girl, so you go adult, while we go play." I'm so glad that the kids are going to have a relationship with their sister. It isn't fair to any of them what happened, but they all need this bonding.

So, Carson said go adult, right? If he only knew I was going in for my yearly physical, and to get Caitlynn added to my insurance. Shit, I need a pediatrician for Caitlynn too. I run upstairs to take a shower and clean everything up for my physical.

I get to my doctor's appointment, and they give me a list of the pediatricians to check out. My check-up goes by smoothly, and now, I'm off to the hospital for my check and to ask about some of the pediatricians on this list. When I get there, I'm surprised to see the ER is packed. Luckily, I have extra scrubs here, so I change and call Carson. "Hey bud. I got here, and the ER is packed, and two nurses called off. Can you keep Caitlynn for a while, or do you need me to figure something else out? I don't have any idea, when I'll be done. Which reminds me, I need to find a daycare for her." I say, making a note in my notepad.

"It's cool I've got this. We are going to play at the park for about another thirty minutes, and then go home and take our meds and naps. We will be fine." He is chuckling, and I can hear Caitlynn squealing in delight in the background.

"Yeah, you sure do. I love you, Carson. Shit, someone is calling. I gotta go. Talk to you later."

"Hello?"

"Hey sweetheart. Have you missed me?"

"Oh, hey Maddox. How are you? Shit hang on. I gotta change my shirt." I put my phone down on the bench, so I can change into my scrubs. "Okay, I'm back. What's up?"

"I just wanted to hear your voice and make sure we were still on for tonight?"

"Shit I'm so sorry. I came into work to get my check, and two nurses called in. So, the ones that are here are the same that have been here since yesterday. So, I'm going to work, and I don't know how long I'll be here. Can we reschedule?"

"Yeah, I'm on my way in, so we can work together. I need to see you, and if I can only see you at work, then I guess that will have to do for now."

"Okay, gotta go. See you soon." I click the phone off and drop it in my locker. Rushing out the door, I pull my hair up in a messy ponytail. I get to the counter, grab the first chart, and get to work. I work for four hours and only see Maddox in passing.

Finally, we slow down a little, and I go to grab a bite to eat. Then, I think of Caitlynn, so I head to the locker room and grab my phone.

187

Looking at my screen, there are messages from Carson, and its pictures of Caitlynn eating spaghetti, her in the bath smiling and playing, and then the last one is her snuggled in her crib with her baby doll sound asleep. I smile, as I put my phone back in my purse without even checking any other messages. I head to the restroom to wash up, before grabbing something to eat.

At the vending machine, I grab a couple waters and some crackers with peanut butter. This will have to do. I turn the corner on a mission, but there stands Maddox with a smirk on his face. "Are you looking for someone?"

"Yeah, you. Do you have time for a small dinner of water and peanut butter crackers?"

"Yeah, sweetheart. For you, I have all the time in the world." We walk to the staff lounge, sitting down for our dinner, when our pagers go off. "Do you think maybe someday we will get to have a real dinner together?"

He smiles, placing his hand under my chin softly kissing my lips. "I'm going to keep trying, but I needed to taste your lips." My face instantly turns red.

We turn to walk out, but he pulls my hand, slowing me down, as I look up in question, and he brings his lips down to mine once more. This time his tongue brushes my lips, and when I open for him, he slowly slides his tongue in, kissing me so slowly and thoroughly that I feel my toes tingle. When he lifts his head, he says, "If I can have more kisses, then I can wait for the dinner, but not too long." With a wink, we go our separate ways.

We don't see each other again, and he is able to leave, when first shift gets there. However, I'm asked to stay, because another two nurses called in with the flu. It's constantly busy the entire time, and I don't once sit down. When my supervisor comes in and sees me, I know I'm in trouble. She calls me to her office, but we have a life flight coming in, so she has to wait. Finally, we get the patient stable, sending him for surgery, and I get cleaned up and head to her office.

"Want to explain to me why you are here working for the past twenty hours, when you are still scheduled to be on vacation?" She doesn't look angry just concerned.

"Well Barb, I came in to get my check yesterday, and the place was packed. I mean, there were people waiting outside it was so packed." I explain to her about all the call-ins, and how I didn't think I was doing anything wrong, because I jumped in to help. "I honestly hadn't realized I had been here over twenty hours. We have been that busy."

"We love your dedication and your work performance, but we don't want you to burn yourself out. I'm going to give you three extra days off added to your vacation to make up for this. You can bet your ass I'll be checking to see why I wasn't notified, when my staff called in. That's all for now, so go home and finish your vacation."

"Thank you so much, Barb. You're an awesome boss. Do you happen to have the insurance paperwork, so I can add Caitlynn to my policy?"

"I actually put it in with your check, and she was added last pay period, so she is covered now."

"Thank you so much. I'll see you in a week." I head to the locker room to take a shower and get changed to head home. I grab my travel bag, putting yesterday's clothes on. Lucky for me, I keep extra pair of underwear here along with my scrubs. Grabbing my bag with my dirty clothes, I head out of the door. I don't bother looking at my phone because I know it's dead anyway.

I just need my bed.

Claire

As I sit down in my car, I feel the exhaustion start to hit me. Starting the car, I put my Avenged Sevenfold playlist on full blast, and then head to the closest gas station. I fill up the car and grab me a Pepsi. Hopefully, it will help me stay awake, until I get home.

Finally making it home, I see Carson playing in the backyard with Caitlynn, as Carly and Mom swing on my porch swing. Caitlynn sees me, and her whole face lights up, as she drops her toys and runs to me. My heart literally melts. I don't care how much hurt and anger I have towards her birth parents. I love her, as if I gave birth to her.

She starts wiggling to get down, and we play for about an hour. I know I'm going to crash, and she can go with me, so we can cuddle on my bed. As soon as we both lay down, we are out.

When I wake up, Caitlynn is laying there, looking right into my eyes. She leans over, whispering, "Hi Mommy. I love you." Holy shit. She just called me Mom. I can play this one of two ways. I can either tell her the truth, or I can play along. Either way, I don't want to hurt her.

"Hi baby. I love you, too. How was your nap?"

"Good. Wanna play with my babies?"

"Sure, I need to go potty, and then we can play." There is a knock on the door, and Carly pokes her head in. "Oh, we were hoping to let you get a little more sleep. Want me to take her, so you can go back to sleep?"

"No, thank you. I'm okay, and we are going to play babies."

"Okay, you silly girls. I'll see you downstairs in half an hour for lunch." I grab Caitlynn up, and we rush down the hall towards her room, as she laughs. I missed this so much. It's been a long time, since I've taken care of a child this small.

After a while, I hear someone clear their throat, and when we look up, Carly is standing there tapping her foot. "Oops. Guess we lost track of time." We head downstairs with our babies because Caitlynn insists on feeding them. Half way through lunch, I yawn, and Carly asks Caitlynn if she wants to go to the park and play for a little while.

"Can I take my baby?"

Man, she is so funny. Carly pretends to think about it, and finally gives in, making both of us giggle. I hug and kiss them both on the head, and then go upstairs to finish my nap.

When I wake up again, it's almost dark out. I get up, grab a quick shower, and head downstairs. I stop and stare, as Maddox sits with Molly, Morgan, Ben, Janelle, Frank, Pete, Carly, Xavier, my mom, and Carson with Caitlynn on his lap. It feels strange that he's in my house, but also good at the same time. Caitlynn sees me, and she jumps down, running at me full speed, and I brace myself, scooping her right up. *God, I love this girl.* She gives me Eskimo kisses, as she whispers yells, "I love you and have missed you so berry much. Can we go to the park morrow?"

"Yes, sweet girl. If it doesn't rain, we can go to the park. Shall we see what's for dinner?"

"You're silly, Mommy. Carson made steaks on the drill. Did you know it's a boy's job to cook on the drill, and a girl's job to cook on the stove? I want a drill, so I can cook on both."

"First off baby, it's a grill, and we will see about getting you one. Second, that is wrong. Both girls and boys can cook on a grill or on the stove. Let's go eat, baby girl."

"Mommy, can I sit by you and Maddox? Did you know he doesn't get to play at the park a lot? I told him he can come wif us. Is it, kay?"

Chuckling at the excitement of her talking a mile a minute, I say, "Yes baby, that's fine."

We sit down next to Maddox, and Carson tries to get Caitlynn to sit with him, so I can eat, but she is having none of that. Everyone is talking and enjoying themselves. After a while, I look down, seeing Caitlynn asleep on my lap, and Maddox smiles, as he whispers, "Why didn't you call or text me back? I was so worried."

"Shit, I'm so sorry. I haven't even plugged my phone in. It was dead, when I finally got off work. When I got home, we played, and then took a nap. I'll be right back. I need to put her in bed and plug my phone in." As I make my way through the house and up to Caitlynn's room, I pull out her pajamas and a pull-up. He comes up behind me, whispering, "Won't this wake her?"

"Not if I do it right." After I get her changed and laid down, we just stand by the crib, looking at her. "She looks like an angel, but I can promise, if we wake her, she is the devil."

He laughs. "I think we are all a little like that."

Leaving her room, we go into mine, and I grab my phone out of my bag, plugging it in. I feel him move behind me, as he wraps his arms around me. I'm trying to decide what I'm feeling right now. It's something I haven't felt in a very long time if ever. I lean my head back on his chest, as he says, "I want you in a way I haven't wanted anyone. I have to be honest with you again. I have been with my share of woman, and I won't even try to lie to you. I've tried to have relationships. However, you know my hours and not everyone can handle them. There was always something missing too, and I just figured I was expecting too much, but when I saw you, it was like my soul recognized its other half. So again, I want you, but not just for the night or the weekend. I want you for the long haul, but I don't just want you though. I want Caitlynn, Carson, and Carly also. I know you can't have more kids." He must see the shock on my face. "I pay attention, and I'm perfectly fine with that. I figure we have Caitlynn, and any grandkids Carson and Carly give us, but just so you know, Caitlynn will *never* date." He stops for a minute, letting me take it all in, before he continues.

"I know this is a lot to take in, and I don't want to scare you. I'm just trying to start this off right, and the best way to do that is to be honest. I know you've had problems in the past, but I don't want you to ever doubt how I feel about you.

I let out a giggle, as I turn around in his arms. "I'm not going to lie I'm scared, and not of you, but of my feelings and getting hurt. I don't want to lose myself again. I want you for as long as we both still feel like this, but I need you to promise me something. If you find someone else or decide you want out, please just tell me first. Don't cheat on me."

"I can promise you that I won't feel that way, or even want anyone the way I want you, but I promise I'll tell you, if that changes."

"Thank you." I stand on my tiptoes and kiss him slowly. I lick the seam of his lips, as he opens his mouth slowly, and then I brush my tongue against his. We stand like that just kissing, until my phone goes off. I look over, and I'm shocked to see I have over seventy-five missed calls and fifty text messages. He chuckles, "I bet a lot of those are from me. I told you I was worried."

Sitting on my bed, we listen to the messages, and then I get to one that makes my world start spinning. It's my OBGYN's office calling to tell I need to come in, as soon as possible for some testing. I'm literally freaking out inside. I hang up the phone, holding onto Maddox a little tighter. His hold tightens around me, as I whisper, "Please stay."

"Try to make me leave." I could really see myself falling for this man.

"I know this is a little fast, but I really need you right now."

"I need you too, sweetheart. More than you know." When we curl up in bed together, my body instantly relaxes, as I drift off to sleep.

When I wake up, I feel him next to me, and I roll over, looking at his face. He truly is beautiful. Very carefully, I roll out of bed, grabbing my phone, before I make my way to the bathroom. I make the call to the doctor's office, and they tell me to be in an hour. I will give myself, until this shower is over, to feel stressed and nervous. Then, I will pull up my big girl panties and calm down. No matter what the test says, and no matter what happens in my life I have three kids to fight for. I get out and dry off. As I finish my routine, I quietly walk back to my room.

"Were you just going to leave me here without a word?"

"Oh, my goodness. You scared the hell out of me. No, I wasn't going to leave without waking you first. I needed a shower and to call some doctors back about myself and Caitlynn. Now that I have done those things and you're awake, I can get dressed and head to our appointments."

"Please let me in. I'm not trying to take control. I just want to be involved."

I nod head, "I will try, I promise. It's just hard because I've been doing it by myself now for a long time."

Groaning, he says, "Babe, you dropping that towel isn't helping my decision to go slow."

Brushing my lips on his, I feel bold, and my body is turned on, so I whisper, "Who said anything about slow? I want you." He picks me up by my ass, as I wrap my legs around his waist, and he stalks towards the bathroom. While he turns on the shower, I lock the door. "I already locked your bedroom door."

"You realize I just showered, right?"

"Looks like you are taking another one." He throws me a quick smirk.

Never losing eye contact, he starts to take his clothes off, and watching him get undressed is literally setting my inside on fire. I step into the shower, as our eyes are still locked together, and I start palming my tits and pulling my nipples. Still watching him, I run my hand down my body and rub my fingers around my lips, drawing a moan out of him and me. Dipping my fingers inside my heat, I move them to where I need them. Being without a man for so long, I learned how to take care of myself.

Finally, when Maddox can't take it anymore, he comes into the shower with me, grabbing my wrist and putting my fingers in his mouth, as we both moan. Our eyes are still on each other, as he slowly lets my fingers drop from his mouth, replacing them where mine were just at. He starts thrusting his fingers in and out of me, and I reach out, stroking his cock. Our eyes stay connected the entire time, as we both find our release together. We rinse off, and I get out and dry off. When he comes out of the bathroom, he grabs a duffle bag and pulls clean clothes out. I just lift my brow in question, and he shrugs. "With my hours, I always carry it in my car." I nod my head in understanding.

I wrap my arms around him, kissing him softly, "I'll call you later, okay?"

"Yeah, and we can meet up here and get Caitlynn, and then go to the park and play." At my confused look, he gets a cocky look on his face. "You still owe me a date."

Cheeky bastard.

Claire

When I get to the doctor's office, he decides that he wants to run a couple more tests, before he gives me any details. He found a few things he wanted to look closer at, so before giving me a diagnosis, he wants to make sure everything is right. So, I make an appointment to come back Monday. Leaving there, I grab Caitlynn and take her to the pedestrian's office, and they tell me she is a very healthy little girl and is one hundred percent on track to where she needs to be. At least Clarissa was doing something right.

Leaving there, we go to get some food and take it to the park. I call Maddox, letting him know where we are, and that I have food. As I swing Caitlynn, I spot him in blue jeans and an orange t-shirt stretched across his chest. *Damn, he looks sexy.* Spotting us, he waves and heads in our direction. As soon as he walks up, he bends down on his knee, "Caitlynn, what is the first thing we should do?"

She squeals. "The swings silly, and Mommy can push you all the way into the clouds!"

"Alright, let's get to the clouds." I gently push on his back the same way I do hers, and she giggles.

"Mommy, he's big. You gotta push him hard."

"No baby. He is going high enough."

Thirty minutes later, we finally talk Caitlynn into eating. Sitting on a blanket under a tree, while eating our subs, she talks about everything we did today. Carly calls to tell me that my mom is still not feeling well, and she truly thinks she should be checked out, but Mom is being stubborn and refuses to go. When we finish at the park, I tell Maddox about Mom, and he follows us to my house to check her over.

Her blood pressure is kind of high, but she says it's because she's ready to go home. I agree because I can't make her enjoy living where I do, and I'd rather her be happy than anything, so the kids are going to take her home tomorrow. She wants to leave Caitlynn here for now, until she feels better. We had originally planned to split up visits, but as long as she is sick, then I think it's best if she stays as well. Once the commotion has calmed down, we have a relaxing night, making homemade pizza, and Mom even sits at the table talking with us, while we make some cookies and candies.

Finally, we all go to bed, and again, Maddox is in bed with me. I could really get used to this. I know we are moving a little fast, but this really does feel right with him. The next morning, I get up early and make breakfast for everyone, before they hit the road. Carly is driving Mom in her car, while Xavier drives his truck, so Carly has a way home. For some reason,

I have this nagging feeling something bad is going to happen, but I just can't put my finger on what it is. I try to let it go, but it continues to linger long after they leave.

******

Caitlynn and I spend the next three days together checking out day-care centers. She has only liked one so far, and that is probably where I'll put her. Lucky for me, it's at the hospital, and they are there for all shifts. However, if it's possible, and I'm working third shift, Carson or Carly will stay home with her. I finish filling out all the forms, making sure I put the kids down, as they may pick her up or drop her off from time to time.

Maddox has come over for dinner every night, and usually, he stays the night. Carly and Xavier should be back today, so I'm going to make their favorite dinner, which is tacos. I decide, since it's such a nice day out, to push Caitlynn in a wagon to the grocery store. Getting everything, we need, and plus some extra snacks, we make our way home.

While I'm making dinner, I hear a car pull in, and I run to the door, so excited that they are both back and safe. I still have that nagging feeling something bad is about to happen, but I'm trying to let it go. Molly keeps telling me I'm over thinking everything. Morgan also received all the paperwork, listing me as Mom's power of attorney, and as the legal guardian for Caitlynn. I know Clarissa wanted Mom to take fully custody, but we decided I should be the one just in case. So, at least that is all settled.

Wrapping my arms around Carly and Xavier, I hug them both. I'm so happy they are both back home safe and sound.

Claire

The next day my world is shattered with a simple phone call. My mom died of a heart attack, during the middle of the night. I knew the feeling that I had was a warning, and now, I'm a complete mess. I'm not sure how I get myself and Caitlynn packed and ready to go within the hour, but somehow, I do. I hear the knock on the door, and I'm frozen in place. I'm so afraid that it's more bad news. Afraid that I'm going to lose Caitlynn. Afraid something else has happened to someone that I love, and once again, I'm going to be left alone. That is my biggest fear that I'm going to die alone. *I let my mom die alone.* I should have made her stay, and I could have fought more, instead I just let her go. She wasn't even home a twenty-four hours. If I had made her go to the doctor, we could have prevented all of this.

God, I'm so sorry, Mom. I wish I could make you come back to me. I'm so angry.

She was literally the kindest person ever. Why do all of the bad things keep happening to me? I work my ass off and take care of my kids, but I can't catch a break. She was more than my mom, she was my best friend, and my person. The one I call when something goes right or even wrong. She was my everything, and now, she's just gone.

The knock comes again, bringing me out of my thoughts. *Time to be an adult.* Thankfully, it's just my neighbor, telling me he can watch the house, while we are gone. We are leaving around four a.m., so Caitlynn can sleep for a while.

I send Maddox a text, as we get ready to leave. I wish I could ask him to join us, but it's so last minute, and he must work. Speaking of work, when I call to let them know what has happened, they give me three weeks off to get everything taken care of. I miss my mom so much already. Xavier asks if I want him to drive, and Carson snickers, telling him to get in the back with Carly.

"Well, she is upset, so I don't want her to have a breakdown, while driving." Xavier states almost apologetic.

"I have to drive, so I focus on not having a breakdown." I wrap my arms around him, "Thank you. Not only for offering to drive, but also for coming with us. I know Carly is going to need you."

My Escape has three rows, so the very back is where Carly and Xavier are sitting, Caitlynn is in the middle, and Carson is up front with me. Looking in my rear-view mirror, I have to laugh because everyone, but me, has their ear buds in listening to something different. We drive for about five hours, before I need to stop and change Caitlynn and feed everyone.

It Begins with Goodbye

******

Finally arriving at Mom's house, I walk in, expecting to see her walk out of the kitchen and meet us at any second. In my head, I know she will never do that again, but my heart is a completely different matter.

The next day I go to the funeral home, finding out she had her funeral pre-arranged. It's times like this I wish I had my sister to ask for help to make decisions, like keeping the house, clothes, and personal belongings. Carly and Carson have Caitlynn for the day, as I have no idea how long I'm going to be.

After running around for most of the day, I finally get back to the house, seeing Colton standing outside. Great, just what I fucking need today. "Oh, Claire. I'm so sorry about your mom. You know I loved her, as if she were my own."

"Yes, Colton I do know. You can show your appreciation tomorrow at the viewing. If you will excuse me, I need to take care of some other things, before my kids get back."

"Well, that's the other thing I wanted to talk to you about. I want to see all of my kids."

"I'm going to be honest with you here, okay? Carson and Carly are both over eighteen, so I can't make them do anything. Also, you and Clarissa signed away all of your rights to Caitlynn, so you have no right to even think of her as yours."

"This is exactly why I had to turn to other women, including your sister. You're such a bitch to me. Caitlynn is my daughter, and if I decide I want to see her, I should be allowed to, as well as Carly and Carson."

Just then, Carson walks around the corner of the house. "Mom, I called Carly and asked her to take Caitlynn to the park, until we come to get them." He makes sure I'm okay, and then he turns on his dad.

"Colton, you need to back the fuck away from my mom right now. You lost all respect from me, when you cheated her and got Aunt Clarissa pregnant. If that wasn't bad enough, you go and make things even worse by signing Caitlynn away, as if she is nothing more than a junk car or something that you decided you didn't want anymore. Here is a newsflash for you, we are humans. We deserve more from you than when you decide you want to play at being a parent. Now, I think it's time for you to go. Have a safe trip home."

Carson wraps his arm around me, as we walk in the house. He shuts the door behind us, keeping his arms wrapped around me. "I'm sorry he was here today."

"No need for you to apologize, baby. His actions are on him. What do you say we go get your sisters, and then go find some food?"

After picking the girls up, we head to one of my favorite restaurants. Walking inside, I'm hit with tons memories. It's good and bitter sweet all at the same time.

Finally, we arrive back at Mom's house for the night. I toss and turn with thoughts of what I could have done differently. Should I have stayed here in Michigan? Should I have pushed her to stay with me? I shouldn't have added more stress on her for the way Colton and Clarissa acted.

I finally get up, knowing that I'm not going to sleep anyway, and I start going through Mom's closet. *Jeez, she has a lot of clothes.* Most of which, I'm going to donate to the local women's shelter. I guess these next few days are strictly up to me.

******

It's time for my mom's viewing, and I want to lock myself in the bathroom and cry all day. I don't want to do this. I want her to still be here, but I know she would want me to put on a brave face. Pulling the dress over my head, I slip my feet into the ballet flats and go get Caitlynn ready. This is one of the hardest things I've ever done, and I'm only a quarter of the way done with it.

It Begins with Goodbye

Caitlynn has been pretty good in the stroller with her toys, and Carly has been with her most of the day. Finally, I'm through with visitation today, and now, the next step is not breaking down tomorrow. I don't know how to say goodbye to her, and I don't want to. How do I leave the cemetery, knowing that she won't be coming with me? My ringing phone brings me back to reality, and I look down, seeing it's Maddox. I wonder how he knew I needed to talk to him?

"Hello." "Hey babe. How are you?"

"Honestly?"

"Yes, please."

"I'm a basket case, and I'm not sure I'm going to survive this."

"I'm so sorry you are going through this."

"I know, and I'm sorry for being such a baby. I just wish you could be here with me, but I know you need to be there for work."

"What if I could be there with you? Would you be mad at me?"

"No, I'd be so happy that I'd have someone to lean on."

"Well, in that case, I'm in your driveway now. Carson called me, and here I am."

Pulling into the driveway, I slam the truck in park and run into his arms. For the first time, since I got the call about my mom, I feel safe. I'm on an emotional overload. "Maddox, you have no idea how happy I am to see you and to have you here with me for tomorrow. I'm not going to lie. I'm probably going to be a hot mess."

He wraps his arms around my neck and presses my face up with his thumbs. "You have a right to be upset, but you are my hot mess, and I don't care." Hearing someone clear their throat, I feel Maddox tense up. I'm afraid to turn and look, but my curiosity gets the best of me. When I do turn, I wish I wouldn't have.

"What the fuck do you want now, Colton. I thought we went over everything yesterday."

"I was hoping we could talk and try to make things work out between us. I was wrong, and I know it. I'm sorry."

"Oh, my God. Are you serious, right now? We are over, and you are married again to my twin, whom you had a baby with, and then signed her over, like she was a piece of garbage. There is nothing for you and me to ever even think of making work. We are so done."

"We were so good together, and we had a lot of more good times than bad. Can't we give it one more time for the kids?"

"No, Colton. I'm done. We had more good times than bad because I choose to ignore all the bad times and not dwell on them. I'm with Maddox now, and no, I won't leave him and give you another chance. I don't cheat either. That is your specialty. I'm going to lay my cards out for you right here and right now. So, please listen and listen well, as I don't want to see you ever again. I would rather spend an hour in his arms than a year with you, because with him, I know where I stand, and that is right next to him. The very best place in the world to be is in the arms of someone who will not only hold you at your best, but they will pick you up and hug you tight at your weakest moment. And yes, I have that with Maddox. You made choices that affected everyone's lives, yet you want everyone to feel sorry for you. I feel nothing for you, which is very sad, and you would think, after being married to you for years, that I'd feel something, but there is nothing. I hope you can fix your relationship with Carly and Carson, but you and I will never be anything. As for Caitlynn, you signed her away, so again, that ship has sailed. I would say I wish you the best, but I don't wish you anything. I just want you out of our lives. You nor Clarissa neither one showed up for the visitation, and I doubt you will for the funeral, so it's best to leave now and never come back here."

It Begins with Goodbye

While holding hands with Maddox, we walk in the house, and Caitlynn comes running for both of us. "Mommy and Mad, I missed you guys. You were gone forever." I pick her up, squeezing her tight, as I shut the door with Colton standing there watching the whole thing. Hopefully, the door to the past is shut permanently.

******

Today is the day we lay my mom to rest, and I feel like I'm having an out of body experience. This should not be happening to me. As quietly as possible, I go to the bathroom, lock the door, turn the Spotify on, get in the shower, and cry. I'm not sure how long I stay in there, before I feel his arms around me, holding me, rocking me, and whispering that everything will be okay. Finally, I'm all cried out, and we get out and dry off. "Wait, I locked the door."

Looking at Maddox, I raise my eyebrow, "Babe, a butter knife will open locks. Besides, are you really mad? I felt like you needed me more than you needed to be alone." How does always know exactly what to say?

"I just don't know what to do. Do I keep this house or sell it? What about all the stuff she has?"

"Babe stop stressing. Didn't you say you go see her lawyer in the morning? We'll see what her wishes were, and then we will go from there, okay?"

"Okay, thank you."

I blow dry my hair out, put my dress on, a small amount of makeup, and then straighten my hair, well what I can reach, and Carly does the rest. Once we reach the funeral home, I head to the front to see her one more time. I know she can't hear me, but I tell her everything that's happened, how I'm feeling, and how much I wish she was back.

The funeral director comes over, telling me people are starting to show up. "Well Mom, here we go. I hope you know that I will always love you, and please, take care of us down here." After that, I kinda go into auto pilot mode.

It Begins with Goodbye

We greet people, who cared so much about my mom, and they tell us some stories about her. Once it's time to go, I'm still standing at the head of her coffin, when Carson walks up to me. "Come on, Mom. We have to go to the cemetery now."

We head to the graveside service, and then everyone leaves to go to a luncheon. I don't care about food right now. I just want to stay here. I stand here for I don't know how long in the pouring rain just looking at the stone she shares with my dad. I'm left with guilt that she's gone, and I'm still here. I feel lost because she was more than my mom she was my best friend, and the last family I had left. Maddox comes over under an umbrella, holding Caitlynn, snapping me out of my little moment. "I guess it's time for me to go, Mom. I'm sorry, and I love you."

Once we reach the luncheon, everyone stops me, trying to talk, and Caitlynn is getting cranky. Maddox notices, and he takes her to play in the back corner. After visiting for a while, I start to feel bad. I'm shivering, sneezing, and coughing, and I just want to go lay down. After we make it home,

Caitlynn and I curl up, watching a movie together. I lean my head back, closing my eyes for a second, and the next thing I know, someone is taking Caitlynn from me, and I have something shoved into my mouth.

"It's okay. Carly is putting Caitlynn in her bed, and I'm taking your temp. I've noticed you aren't feeling too good," Maddox whispers.

Of course, I have a temp of one hundred and one point nine, so I take two Tylenol, and Maddox draws me a bath. I'm only in there about ten minutes, and then I'm done. I feel the exhaustion taking over my body, and I'm not sure, if I'm strong enough to make it out of the bathroom.

Maddox hears me and comes to help. I get into bed, but I keep waking myself up shivering. The next morning I'm no better, so Carly calls my old family doctor, and he gets me in, so I can get some medicine. Maddox takes me, and they send me for a chest X-ray. I have a sinus infection and pneumonia, and believe me, my body is feeling it. Once I get a shot of antibiotic in my hip, and then two more for home, I get ready to head to the lawyer's office.

Claire

When we get to the office, I find out that anything that Carly, Carson, or myself doesn't want is to be sold, including the house. The money is going to be split between me and the kids. I also get a huge shock, when I find out my mom has a life insurance policy, and she has already set up an account for each of the kids with the same amount of money. Apparently, I'm now one hundred thousand dollars richer. I don't know if it's the sickness or the shock of the money, but I pass completely out.

I don't know how long I'm out, but when I wake up, Maddox is leaning over me, making sure

I'm okay. Finally, opening my eyes, I whisper, "Did that really just happen?"

"Which part? You inheriting money, passing out, or being sick? The answer is all of the above, so I think it's time for me to get you home and in bed."

The lawyer says, "I will have all the paperwork ready to be signed on Monday morning."

"I have one request, before we go. I would like the money from all sales to be divided equally between the women's shelter and for children in foster care please." My mother was very active in the women's shelter by cooking food, buying blankets, and spending the night to help out the workers. Children in foster care was something dear to her, as she was a child in the system, until she was eighteen.

"I'll get that written into the paperwork as well."

"Okay, sounds good, and I'll have her here."

When we finally get home, he again draws me
another bath, because I've been sweating so much.
When I'm done, he helps me in the bed and gives me
my meds. I also manage to eat a couple of crackers,
before I fall sleep.

I wake up the next morning in a sweaty and
sticky mess. Looks like the fever is still breaking. I
roll out of bed, looking at Maddox, and he looks
tired. I decide not to wake him, as I get in the shower.
I'm feeling a little better, but I'm still so exhausted. I
don't even have the energy to rinse the shampoo out
of my hair. Lucky for me, Maddox steps in to help
me. "Babe, why didn't you wake me?"

"I'm sorry. You looked so tired, and I thought
I'd be okay."

"You know I'd have gotten up and helped
you." He sits me down on the bench, rinsing my hair,
while I try to wash my body. Finally, he takes the
washcloth and finishes, and then rinses me from
head to toe. I watch, as he washes his body, and then
gets out. He wraps the towel around me and puts me

in the chair, while he changes the sheets and pillow cases. He helps me get dressed, and then I eat some soup, take my meds again, and then go right back to sleep.

I feel Caitlynn climb next to me, as I open my eyes, and Maddox is lying in bed with us watching Paw Patrol. I move, and she sees I'm awake, and her smile takes up her whole face. We lay in bed all day watching cartoons and just hanging out. It's exactly what I need. Carly, Carson, and Xavier join us as well, and I manage to eat dinner at the table with everyone. I try to give Caitlynn a bath, and I'm good for most of it, until it's time to take her out. Maddox helps, and together we take her to bed.

Lying in bed with Maddox, later that night, he whispers, "I really like this." Giving him a questioning look, he continues, "Me being here with you all the time. I'd like to wake up to your face every morning and go to sleep next to you every night. I think I'm falling in love with you, Claire." He softly says, kissing my lips.

"First, thank you for taking such good care of me the last few days. I honestly couldn't have done it without you. Second, I also like you being here with me, so maybe, you can move in with Caitlynn and me? Carly lives with Xavier, and Carson has his own place."

Placing his forehead on mine, he whispers, "Are you sure? I don't want my heart to be broken."

"I can't promise I'll never hurt you, or make you angry, because I will. I can promise to be faithful and to always tell you, if I don't like something. I wouldn't ask you to move in, if I wasn't sure. I'm falling for you and Caitlynn loves you, so we want you here."

As I'm dozing off, I hear, "When we get married, would you be okay with me adopting Caitlynn, and us raising her as our own?"

"Of course, I want you to adopt her and give her your last name."

"Babe, it's going to be our last name."

It Begins with Goodbye

I can't believe after I spent so many years with an ass-hat that I've finally found my prince charming. As I lay here in his arms, I realize for the first time in my life I feel cherished. It's the best feeling in the world.

Monday morning, I wake up, feeling so much better. Maddox and I go to the lawyer's office to sign everything, and then we are headed back home. I wanted to get everything done in Mom's house this week, but it looks like it's going to take a while to finalize everything.

******

One month later

I stand in the middle of what use to be my mom's house, but it's now just a house with empty walls. It's been a long month, but finally, everything is done, and we can all move on. My only hope is that the next owners have as many wonderful memories as I do.

Opening my eyes, I see Maddox on his knee in front of me with Carly, Carson, Xavier and Caitlynn, standing behind him. Clearing his throat, he says, "I have lived the past forty-one years of my life without you, and I have to say I've only been going through the motions of living. The moment you walked into my life I knew without a shadow of a doubt that you were the one for me to spend the rest of my life with. My soul recognized its other half. I know we have both been through problems, but I promise to give this marriage my all. I want to spend the rest of my life with you, and I want to wake up and go to sleep with you every night by my side. I want to raise Caitlynn with you, and I want to play with all of our grandchildren together. I guess what I'm saying is Claire Renee Mercier will you do me the honor of being my wife, my partner, my lover, and my best friend for all the days of our lives?"

"Yes, Maddox. A thousand times yes. I'll marry you today, and every day for the rest of our lives."

"How would you like to fly to Vegas and get married tonight? We can have our honeymoon for four days, and then head home?"

"Okay, I'm game. Let's go get married."

We fly into Vegas, and he has already rented rooms for everyone. Carly and Carson are taking turns with Caitlynn every other night. Xavier tried to get Carly to marry him today as well, but she refused, because she wants her own wedding.

It's finally time for me to join Maddox in the chapel. Carson and Carly are standing up with us, and Xavier and Caitlynn are next to them. We say the normal vows, and when the minister asks for the rings, I freeze. *Oh my, how could I forget the rings.* Maddox turns, and Carson gives him a ring. Feeling Carly tap my shoulder I turn, and she hands me a wedding band Looking into Maddox's eyes, he winks at me, when I look down noticing they match.

As the tears fall freely from my eyes, I realize I had to go through hell to get my very own piece of heaven, and that is what Maddox is. *My own piece of heaven.* The minister announces us, as Mr. & Mrs. Maddox Field, and I'm so excited.

We all go to change, and then go out to dinner, as a family to celebrate. Carson informs us that he found a petting zoo to take Caitlynn to, so we could be alone. I really do love my little family.

Hand in hand, we walk back to the hotel, as Maddox whispers, "Babe, I'm nervous. This feels like my first time."

I kiss his lips. "It is your first time, as my husband, and nothing before tonight matters." Still hand in hand, we walk to our room, and he lifts me into his arms so easily, carrying me into the room. "Yes, I'll do that again, when we get home to our house."

We kiss, as he slowly slides me down his hard body, until my feet hit the floor. I try to pull his shirt up, as he steps back and whips it over his head.

Walking back to me, he twirls his finger, so I turn, and he starts unzipping my dress. Once he gets so far, I take over, looking at him over my shoulder, as I drop my dress to the floor. He has pure lust all over his face, as I stand here in nothing at all. His eyes to take their leisurely path up and down my body, and I feel so loved and cherished, and he hasn't even touched me yet.

Finally, he walks to me and gently picks me up, as he lays me on the bed. Standing up, he slowly begins to unbutton his pants, sliding them down with his boxers, as I get my fill of looking at him in all his glory. I reach for him, and he comes to me willingly. We slowly kiss and explore each other's bodies, as we find what makes us sigh, moan, and whimper. When he finally enters me, we both moan, as our eyes lock. "It feels like coming home."

"Yes, babe. It does, and it will forever. This is my promise to you." We make slow love all night long.

Waking up the next morning, the reality of what I've done comes crashing down on me. I just don't want to get hurt again. "You about done freaking out?" He asks, standing in the doorway.

"Yeah, I think so. Sometimes I need to not think, but then again, maybe that is what got me here in the first place."

"Let's see if we need to call Morgan to end this, or if we are going to make it work out."

I start to panic, "You want out already?"

"No, but I also don't want to go into this with you having so many doubts, so let's talk this out, okay?"

"Maddox, I truly love you, and that is not why I'm freaking out. Please believe that. I just want us to work, and I'm letting my past cloud my mind. I know we are meant to be together forever." I barely get forever out, before his lips crash down on mine.

Pushing him back against the wall, I fall to my knees, taking his rock-hard cock into my mouth, and swirling my tongue around him, as I take him as deep as I can. He wraps his hands in my hair to guide me, while his hips are pumping in my mouth. He tightens his hands in my hair, letting me know he's close, so I suck harder. His come hits my tongue, and I take every drop of him down my throat, and with his deep voice, he growls my name.

Once he catches his breath, he picks me up, carrying me to the bed. Laying me down, he attacks me, like a man starved. Right as I'm on the edge of the biggest climax of my life, he moves away, as I groan in frustration, and he chuckles. "I've got you, babe," he says, as he slams his rock-hard cock inside of me. It only takes a couple of thrusts, until I'm screaming out my orgasm. He slows down, while I come down, and once I'm back, he starts thrusting harder and faster, and soon, I'm orgasming again, and this time with him. Cuddling with him, we doze off together.

Waking up to a pounding on the door, I jump up to answer it. Molly stands there smiling, "You bitch! You couldn't even call and tell me. You had to get married without me?"

"I'm sorry. It was last minute. Plus, it was just Maddox, the kids, and me. Please, don't be mad."

"I'm not. Just know that you are stuck with me today. We are having a girls' day."

"In case you didn't know, today is my first day as Maddox's wife, and I'm not sure if I'm even leaving this room."

"Yes, you are because we are having a surprise for you tonight. So, kiss your husband, and let's go." Turning around, Maddox stands there with that trademark smirk on his beautiful face. "Go ahead and have a good day, and I'll see you later. No questions though, and I have already told them what is going to happen." I look at him with questions in my eyes.

Shaking his head, he says, "Trust me please." I agree, and then turn to go into the bathroom to get dressed. Coming out, I see Maddox is gone, as Molly says, "He has things to do like we do, so let's roll." Smiling, we leave together arm in arm.

It Begins with Goodbye

The first stop is the spa. We both get manicures and pedicures, as well as the full spa treatment. Surprise number one is not just Molly and me, but also Janelle, Carly, and Caitlynn. We're all laughing and talking, while the ladies do our nails and make-up, but then she covers my mirror. Sensing my distress, Molly says, "Calm down. She knows what's going on and what to do."

After a while, I think I'm ready, until Molly says, "Come on. Let's get you in this dress."

"Where did the dress come from?" I'm really starting to panic now.

"Claire didn't Maddox tell you no questions. Now, we all know what's going on, so let him do this for you, okay?"

"Okay, I guess, but I don't really have a choice."

Finally, she dresses me in a pale-yellow strapless dress that stops just before my knees. She steps back to look, as I see her wipe tears from her eyes. "Are you, okay? Is something wrong?"

"You just look beautiful, and you are so lucky that you have an amazing man."

"Thank you. You kinda had me worried for a minute."

When they let me in front of the mirror, I stop and stare at myself. *I am beautiful.* My hair is pulled up on the left side with a silver barrette, and I have a bump on the back of my head, while the rest is down in curls.

Turning I see that Molly, Carly, and Caitlynn all match me. We take a few pictures, before we make our way downstairs. All the guys are waiting for us, wearing khaki pants and pale blue shirts.

Maddox comes over and gives Caitlynn a necklace that says my princess, as he kisses her on the check. He hands me a bouquet of daisies, and my heart melts right there. Offering me his arm, he says, "Shall we?"

We walk into a banquet type room, and the song *"Heartbeat"* by Carrie Underwood is playing, and Maddox takes my hand, leading me to the dance floor. As we dance to the song, I realize how perfect it is for us.

I lean my head on his chest and listen to his heartbeat. I know this is like our wedding reception, and I realize this is the most romantic thing anyone has ever done for me. I am in awe of this man that loves me so completely. We didn't have the normal or traditional relationship from the start, but at the end of the day, there is no one I'd rather have by my side than him. I hope I make him as happy as he makes me.

Once our song is over, the next song one plays, as everyone joins us on the dance floor. Looking around, I see some of our friends from the hospital, as well as Maddox's parents here. He really went all out. Caitlynn comes up to dance with Maddox and me. Next, Carson steps up, and I let him take the lead.

"Mom, you look so beautiful. If I had any ounce of doubt that he wasn't the man for you, I wouldn't have given my blessing. I love you, and I'm so grateful that you opened your heart to love again. Just remember though, if Maddox messes up, I will be there to kick his ass," he says, making sure Maddox hears him.

Maddox just smiles. "If I'm ever dumb enough to hurt your mom, you have my permission to kick my ass."

Then Carson gets all serious. "Sorry you had to waste all those years on a loser."

"Carson Phillip, I may have not had the best marriage, but it gave me you, Carly, and Caitlynn. So yes, it ended, and it wasn't good, but I don't regret it, because it gave me you three kids, and I love you more than anything else. If I had to do it all over again, I'd do it again just to have you guys."

"I would never wish that on anyone or want anyone to ever live through something like that, but I do love you so much."

"I love you, too, and someday, you will find a girl that will turn your whole world around."

"I already found her, and I'm dancing with her right now."

"Someday you will make someone very happy."

As the night goes on, we dance with everyone, including each other. Around eleven thirty, Carson takes Caitlynn up to bed. I've been looking for Carly for a while now, and finally, I see her, standing alone at the windows. As I turn to tell Maddox I'm going to see her, he picks me up and kisses me slowly. "Leave her be. It's our honeymoon."

Quickly, we leave the reception, heading to our room. Once we get in the elevator, I ask, "Any more surprises?"

"No, and I don't plan on leaving the room tonight or tomorrow. After that, it's up for debate."

"I can get behind that one hundred and fifty percent, as long as the kids don't need us."

"Oh, babe. I've got them covered. You are all mine for the next thirty-six hours."

Kissing his lips, I tell him, "Actually, I'm yours for the next ninety-nine years." We make love all night only stopping to rest for a little while, and then we are right back at each other.

Yeah, it couldn't be more perfect.

Claire

The next morning, we order room service, after we spend several hours pleasing each other. We both lay in bed just talking and getting to know one another more. His phone rings a couple of times, and he looks at the screen and just sets it back down. I'm trying to remind myself that he is not Colton. However, it's hard, as I have been burned before.

Quietly, I get up and go to the bathroom, lock the door, and take a long hot bath. He has knocked a couple times, but I have turned my music up a little louder. After a while, I finally get my head out of my ass and get out ready to apologize only to find him gone. He didn't leave a note or anything.

I call and check in on the kids, and each of them has plans today, so I throw on my running clothes and go to the gym. First stop is the treadmill, and I work myself up to a run. After a while, I hear someone clearing their throat, and I turn to see Maddox standing there. I'm so happy to see him that I completely forget that I was angry. I launch myself at him, and he catches me so easily, as I kiss him hard on the mouth.

When he pulls back, I say, "You left and didn't leave a note. The kids had plans, so I came here." He just looks at me finally saying, "Are you sure that's why you are here?"

"No, I'm here because I'm trying to outrun my past and my issues."

"Babe, I know how hard it was for you, when I didn't answer my phone, and I turned it face down. I wasn't trying to hurt you. It was a surprise for you, when we get home. Speaking of which, who is moving in with who?"

"Umm, I thought you had basically moved in with me already."

He laughs, "Yeah, you're right. I was just checking."

"You're a funny guy. Let's go shower, so we can go see everyone, before they leave."

"Babe, they left already. It's just us and the kids."

Wrapping my arms around him, I say, "As long as I have you, I'll be good to go. So, am I going to be any lady's enemy, when we get home?"

"What are you talking about? Sometimes you confuse me with the things that come out of your mouth."

"You don't have any women you called, when you needed a release? Anyone, I need to worry about slashing my tires, or keying my car?"

"You act as if I'm a prize or something. I'm just a guy, and yes, there were women I called. However, the moment I laid eyes on you I was done. I haven't called, texted, or had any contact with any of them since then."

"Maddox, I was there for two months, before we even talked."

"Yes, dear I know. I went a long time with only my hand for pleasure. Not because I couldn't get anyone, but because you broke him."

I can't help it I bust out laughing.

"Laugh all you want. I couldn't get it up because they weren't you."

"You just made me fall in love with you all over again."

Claire

The following Monday we arrive back at work, and both of us are working different shifts. Maddox is on days, while I'm on nights. Going in to eat my lunch, I see that he has packed me a crunchy peanut butter and grape jelly sandwich, banana, and peanut butter crackers, and at the bottom of my lunch bag, is a note.

> *Babe you got this. I love you.*
> *Maddox <3*

Grabbing my phone, so I can send him a message, I see he will be arriving here in about two hours, so I decide I'll wait. I'm making my way back to the restroom, when my pager goes off, and I run back to the ER. We are swamped for the rest of my shift, and I don't even see Maddox, when he gets here. We are so busy that he leaves a note for me on the counter that Caitlynn is at daycare for the day.

Finally, it's three thirty in the afternoon, and I've been here for nineteen hours. I'm so ready for bed. Maddox drives us home with Caitlynn, chatting happily in the back seat all the way. I ask her what she wants for dinner, and of course, she wants chicken nuggets or pizza.

She's turned into a total daddy's girl now that Maddox has legally adopted her. When we get home, Maddox offers to make dinner, so I can shower and sleep, but Caitlynn informs him that she and I are making him a surprise dinner. Laughing he kisses her softly and agrees. He heads up to take his shower, and we start spaghetti, salad, and garlic bread. Caitlynn is cooking in her kitchen, when the phone rings, and it's Carson asking what's for dinner. I tell him spaghetti, and he says he's on his way.

Hanging up with him, I go back to cooking. When "Take your time" by Sam Hunt comes on, we start dancing around the kitchen. These are the moments I live for. I love that I got to do these silly little things with Carson and Carly, and now, I get to do them with Caitlynn as well. Carson walks in and starts dancing with us, well with Caitlynn, as Maddox grabs me, and we sway to the music. He asks me if I want to sit and rest. "No, because I know as soon as I sit, I'm not going to want to move, and I need a shower and get a couple hours of sleep."

After eating and cleaning up, Caitlynn and I go up to take our nightly baths. It's our time together. Getting out, we decide to both wear nightgowns tonight, and Maddox is sitting on our bed, when we come out. He tells me that Barb called, and I'm off tonight, as I worked today. It works out because I have a doctor's appointment tomorrow.

"Do I need to take the day off and go with you? Why didn't I know you had a doctor's appointment?"

"No, you don't have to go. I've been going to these by myself for several years now. It's for my yearly exams, so you didn't know, because it's no big deal. I actually forgot about it, until my reminder popped up on my phone. Did I answer all of your questions?"

"Babe, why are you getting so defensive?"

"I'm sorry, Maddox. I'm used to doing everything on my own. It's not a big deal."

Leaning over, I kiss him softly, and then he grabs our giggling girl and takes her to her bedroom. I sit down in the rocking chair with her and read her a bedtime story. This is my favorite part of every day, as I sit here with her, and she wraps her finger in my one strand of hair. She tries almost as hard as I do to stay awake. However, the next thing I know Maddox is taking Caitlynn and putting her in her bed, and then picking me up and taking me to bed.

I wake up the next morning and freak out because Maddox is still in bed. "Calm down, babe. I'm on nights for the rest of the week." Then I realize that I haven't heard Caitlynn. Rolling to get out of bed, Maddox tightens his arm around me. "She is already at daycare, so I need to go back to sleep." He sets the alarm for noon, which will give me plenty of time to get to my appointment on time.

After all the thoughtfulness he has shown me this morning, I think he deserves a reward. So, I slide down, taking him into my mouth. He only lets me play for a minute, before he picks me up and sets me down on his cock, and I ride him hard. We are both sated and fall right back asleep.

When the alarm goes off, we get up and shower, and I get ready to go. I ask him if he wants to go with me, and he jumps at the chance. Once we get there, I'm so glad he came with me. I guess life isn't quite done fucking with me yet. "When we did your physical, I felt a lump, which caused me some concern. So, that's why we did the CT scan and more blood work. We have the results in, and you have what is called epithelial cell tumors on your ovaries. This is the most common type of ovarian cancer in women. The good news is so far it hasn't travelled outside of your ovaries. So, I need to send you to an oncologist for further treatment, okay? I'm sorry. I know this is a lot to take in at one time."

"Yeah, it's a lot, but it has to be okay. I mean, I can't freak out because I have a three-year-old at home, and two kids in college. So, let's get this scheduled and going." Checking out, the nurse tells me, "They have made you an appointment with the local oncologist, and it's for tomorrow at two forty-five in the afternoon."

I thank her, and we leave. I honestly don't know how to feel, or even what to feel. I do know I'm very pissed. I mean, I just found Maddox and Caitlynn, and, now, I could die and leave them all alone. I can see Maddox's lips moving, but I don't hear what he's saying I'm so lost in my own head. Looking at where my speedometer is, I see a picture of Carly, Carson, and Caitlynn all together, and it sends so many emotions through me at once.

I know Xavier will take care of Carly, but she's still broken up with him, and I still don't know why. This breaking up is recent, but something major is going on with her, and I need to have some girl time with her. Oh shit, she's gone to that conference this week, and she won't be home until next week one day. I wonder if Xavier got his head out of his ass and went to her, like I told him to.

Before I know it, we make it to the hospital, and I head straight to my supervisor's office. I explain everything, as she says, "We will work with you, and don't worry about your job. You just worry about getting better."

Maddox asks me to wait here, while he goes and talks to his supervisor, but I need to get more blood work. "I'm going to get my blood work done, and then to get our girl. I really need to see her."

Once I'm done, I get her, and Maddox isn't back yet, so we look around the gift shop. Caitlynn is talking about this boy in daycare. "Jack is my boyfriend, and we got married today. Look at my ring, Mommy. It's as big as yours!"

Laughing, I say, "Yes, baby. It is, and it's your favorite flavor watermelon." I look at the ring pop on her finger, as she stands there licking it. "So, what made you decide to marry Jackson, instead of Luke or one of the other boys?"

"Well, he bought me a ring, he sits by me, and he plays with me on the playground. He even shared his snack pack with me, because he got chocolate, and I had vanilla." I feel the air change, as Maddox comes in, but I keep Caitlynn talking.

When she sees him, she yells, "I got married."

"It's time to lock her in the basement now."

"Daddy, your happy and married to Mommy. Why can't I be happy and married to Jack? I love him!"

Oh, my God. This little girl is going to be a handful, when she grows up. She is laughing out loud, as Maddox gives me a dirty look. He comes over, picking her up, "Baby, I told you boys are yucky. We don't like them remember."

"Mommy, did Daddy hurt his head today?"

"No, why?"

"Cause, he says boys are yucky, but he's a boy, and so is Carson and Xavier, and we love them." Just then, someone calls my name, and I'm saved.

Quickly walking over, they tell me they just got another order in for more blood work. Guess I better get used to being stuck all the time. I head over to wait for my turn, as I text Maddox to let him know. I also send Carson and Carly a text, telling them I love them, and we need to have a family meeting soon. Just then, my phone rings, and it's Xavier.

"Hey X. What's up, bud?"

"Claire! She left me, and I don't know what to do."

"What do you mean she left you?"

"Carly did. Hang on, I'll read you the note."

Xavier,

I love you, and I'm not sure that will ever change. However, seeing you at a diner with another woman holding hands has shattered my heart. I'm completely devastated thinking of you with someone else, when I want you for myself. I know I'm selfish, but I don't want you to settle. I want you to be as happy with someone who makes you as happy as you make me, even if that person isn't me. I'm going back to Michigan because it hurts way too much to even think of you with someone else, let alone see it every day. Part of the reason I left the way I did is because I have always promised myself that I would not allow a man to treat me the way my dad treated my mom. You have always treated me like your queen, until I saw you with another woman. I refuse to be second best or the girl you call, when everyone else is busy. I deserve to be someone's one and only, and I refuse to accept less than that from you or anyone. Please know this is the hardest thing I have ever done. I know you will always be a part of our family, but for now, I need space to get my head on straight. Please know, I will always love you, and I love you enough to let you go, so you can find your true happiness.

With all my heart and love,

Carly

"Now, what do I do? She is my happily ever after still and always. Please help me. I was at the diner meeting with the ring designer, picking up her engagement ring. I had to get it resized, after I figured out it was too big."

"Give me ten minutes, and I'll call you back. I gotta get blood work." Hanging up with him, I call Carly, but it goes to straight voicemail, so I know it's shut off. "Carly Lynn, what are you doing? I need to talk to you about something very important. Please call me back, as soon as you get this."

I can't fix this now, so I go and get my blood drawn. *Geez, twelve vials.* I wonder if I have any blood left in my body. Walking out and over to Maddox and Caitlynn, I see they are in a heated conversation. "Daddy, that's not fair! I want to be married to Jack, so please don't make me break up with him."

Oh lord. "Maddox come on and take me home, please. I'm ready for a nap." My phone starts ringing, as we get up to leave.

"Mommy, what's wrong with you? Why do you look so different? Why are you not answering your phone?"

"Caitlynn, give me a second, okay? I look sick, because they took more blood from me, and I didn't answer the phone, because I'm talking to you and your dad. Oh, my God, Maddox. It's the doctor's office. What do you think they want?"

"Babe, answer the phone, and we will know."

"Or I could let it go to voicemail, and then just listen to that."

"Babe give me your phone," I do, and then stand here, listening to everything he says.

"Hello. Yes, this is Claire Fields husband, Maddox. Yes, we will be at the appointment tomorrow. Yes, we can come early and fill out paperwork. She just had lab work done, and they took twelve vials. She also had some before that. Okay, thank you. Yes, see you then."

I'm sitting in a chair with my head between my legs, while Caitlynn is still going on about Jack. I start laughing, because well honestly, I think I'm having a mental breakdown. I think that maybe I'm thinking too much about this, but then again, my whole world feels as though it's crashing around me. However, for my family, I need to be a strong mom and wife. I just need to get my thoughts and feelings down for everyone. As we walk out of the hospital, me on one side holding Caitlynn's hand and Maddox on the other, it hits me that I need to get some family pictures scheduled. I need these memories just in case. Not only for myself, but the kids, too.

When we get home, I tell Maddox about Xavier, and he tells me to call him back, so I do, but he's so upset, as I try to talk some sense into him. "If you love her, then you need to be honest with her and tell her what's going on. Don't let her leave, until she understands you. Also, don't let her second guess herself, or let her get lost in her own head. I love you, and I'm rooting for you and her. When you see her, please tell her we are having a family meeting Monday night here, and I need both of you here, whether your together or not."

"Okay, I love you, and we will be there, I promise." He says, as we hang up.

Sitting on my bed, Caitlynn comes through my door looking pissed. "Baby girl, what's wrong?"

"Daddy said I have to break up with Jack tomorrow. Mom, he doesn't understand. I don't want to break up with him because he's my friend."

"I'll talk to Daddy, okay? Come up here and give me some cuddles. I have missed you." She jumps up on the bed and cuddles up to me. The next thing I know Maddox is putting her in her own bed. When he comes back in, he says, "Looks like my beautiful girls were tired."

"Babe, can you promise me something?"

"I'll try. What's up?"

"Can you promise to move on and fall in love, if I die? I don't want you to be alone forever, and let's face it, you're going to need help with Caitlynn. She is already mad because you won't let her stay married."

"Sweetheart, I can't promise you that, because you're going to live a long life. I promised to always be faithful, until death do us part, and our family is going to be right beside you the whole time. We are fighting this together, and you will beat it."

I open my mouth, but he covers it with his own. "Tonight, is about showing each other what we mean to each other." Slowly, we make love, and as we reach our orgasms together, our eyes lock, and I whisper, "I love you," as a single tear slides down my face.

Waking up in the morning, I get my scrubs on, and get Caitlynn ready for daycare. I better talk to Maddox about this Jack thing, before my girl has a breakdown. "Babe leave her alone about Jack. The more you push her to break up with him the more she's going to stick with him. She just wants to be happy like we are. I think us being together is setting a good example for her."

"Fine, but I don't like it. When she goes to school, it will be an all girl's school, and she's going to be a nun." I laugh, as I kiss his lips. "Whatever gets you through the day."

He grabs my waist, pulling me to him. "The thought that you are mine for the rest of my life gets me through the day. I'll be with you at the appointment today, and every step of the way for that matter. I promise you."

"I don't know what I did so great to deserve you, but I love you so much. Thank you for loving not only me, but my kids also and for never giving up on me."

"I would never give up on you or the kids. You guys are my whole world now."

God, this man knows exactly what to say to make my heart melt.

Claire

Maddox got called in and couldn't make it to my appointment, and Caitlynn is sick, so here I go, putting my big girl panties on, and carrying in my sleeping daughter. The epithelial cell tumor is a stage two and treatable, which is good news, and I'm scheduled to have a complete hysterectomy next Thursday. Then three weeks later, we will start chemo intravenously. One day every eight weeks for six months, and then we will do another CT scan. This will cause hair loss, stomach problems, loss of energy, and my immune system will be down, so it will be easier to get sick.

Just then, Caitlynn starts wailing, so I guess that's my cue to go. We make our way back to the car, and my phone keeps ringing and dinging, signaling text messages. I just ignore it. I'm in a fog, and my only thoughts right now are getting Caitlynn home, so she can rest. Getting her home and settled in my bed with me, I get my notebook and pen. I decide to write a few letters, and my first one is to Caitlynn. I'm trying to have a positive outlook, but I need to be prepared for anything at this point.

My dearest Caitlynn,

I'm so sorry I had to leave you so soon. I love you with every breath in my body and have since the beginning. I hope all of your dreams come true. Don't be too hard on your dad. He is trying, and he loves you so very much. I hope you dance like nobody's watching because really who cares. Sing like nobody's listening because I will be, and your voice is like an angel singing to me.

Love like you have never been hurt, because if you never get hurt, you never really loved, and I want that for you more than anything in the world. Your prince

266

charming will come, when the time is right, so don't rush it. You have the ability to change the world with just a smile. I will always be with you in your heart and in your dreams.

Always remember, I love you and am always with you.

Love,

Mommy

Caitlyn is asleep, so I prop pillows around her and head downstairs to get her medicine. I notice the wedding pictures with the kids and us, and then, I see my favorite one. It's the one of Maddox and I with my head on his chest and him kissing the top of my head with our arms wrapped around each other. I feel such devastation at the fact that he could again lose his wife. I feel an urgency in me to write his letter and let him know that this is also not his fault, and that if I had known that I was going to get sick, I would not have let him fall for me.

267

Maddox,

Please know that you are my dream come true.

The best day of my life is the day we meet. My favorite part is watching the love in your eyes not only for me, but for Carly, Carson, and Caitlynn also. I will always love you. Thank you for taking care of me and loving my kids. I know this sucks, but please find it in your heart to move on. I love you enough to know you deserve to love someone for the rest of your life. Not only for you, but also for Caitlynn. That last sentence is the hardest thing I have ever written. Not only because I had to let you go, but because I'm selfish and want you forever. I don't want some other lady to have what is mine, but I also don't want you to be alone forever. You healed my heart and soul, and for that, I can never repay you.

You are one of the only things that make me feel alive, and I hope we have made enough memories to last, until we see each other again. Please know I'll always be with you. It will get easier, and please remember that with every breath you take. My favorite thing to look at is your smile. My favorite sound to hear is your heartbeat. I love to get lost in your eyes, and I love that we can say so much without making a sound. I'm writing you, so you know how I feel, when I'm not here to say it to you. I hope you know that what we have is all I've ever needed. I'm so truly amazed by your compassion. You made it impossible for me not to fall in love with you, and every day, I thank God for you. You kept knocking my walls down, and I'd try to build them right back up, but you wouldn't let me. I never want to see you unhappy. You inspire me every day to fight, so I can stay here with you for a lifetime. I hope you don't get this for about fifty years. Just know, whenever you get it, that I love you.

Yours always,

Claire

Hearing the door open, I rush to put the notebook away in my drawer, as Maddox walks into our room. His eyes go soft at seeing our little girl sick in our bed. I walk to him and wrap my arms around him. "Babe, I'm so sorry I didn't call you, after the appointment. I was hurt that you couldn't be with me. I know it's not your fault, and I was being selfish. Please forgive me?"

"Sweetheart, there is nothing to forgive. I knew you would be hurt, and I'm so sorry. I really tried." I know he means every word too. Suddenly, Caitlynn wakes up and is still feverish, so I take her to get her in the bath. While in there, it hits me. This could be the last time I get to give her a bath, and I start crying all over again. I try to control myself and wash my face, so Maddox doesn't notice.

As soon as we come out of the bathroom, he sees me and knows. He takes Caitlynn to get dressed, dinner, and medicine. He tells me to take a bath, while he takes care of our girl. I'm in the bath for about twenty minutes, just thinking about getting out, when he walks in and starts taking his clothes off. Our eyes lock on each other, as he gets in. "Tell me what's wrong, so I can make it better."

"Where's Caitlynn?"

"Babe quit stalling. She is asleep in her bed, and I brought the monitor."

"Okay, so you know when the doctor did my pap smear, he felt a lump, and the test came back cancerous, so I have to have a complete hysterectomy, and then I'll start chemo once a week for eight weeks. After six months, we will test again and see how it looks. I will be nauseated, fatigue, I will probably lose my hair, and overall, be a burden on you and the kids. You should probably run, while you can." I smile weakly.

"Do you really think I can leave? Do you think I can shut my feelings on and off like a light switch? Do you not know how much I love you? How I wish I could take the cancer out of your body and put it in mine, so you don't have to feel this or go through all of this? If you really believe that I would leave you, then my heart is completely broken."

"No, Maddox. That is not how I feel at all. I love you and know you love me as well. I know feelings can't be turned on or shut off like that. I wouldn't want you to have the cancer, and I'd want to fight it for you, too."

"Babe, can we just fight it together, like we are meant to? I love you, and I finally found the person who completes me. I don't want to lose you, and I will be there to hold your hand during treatments. I will also hold your hair, while you're tossing your cookies. I want to do *everything* with you and only you, so please let me be that person."

"You're the only person I want to do that stuff with. I love you and only you, too." I launch myself at him, kissing him deep and hard.

Resting my forehead on his, I whisper, "Tonight, we can cry, but tomorrow, no more tears. I don't want to die. I want to grow old with you. There are some hard decisions I must make, and I need to know that you will follow my wishes, even if they break your heart. Tonight though, I just want you to hold me and love me, like it could be our last time."

"Babe, I can promise this will not be the last time we do this. We will live a long and happy life together. I'll follow your wishes for no other reason than it's what you want. We'll take everything a day at a time. Now, let's get clean and go to bed."

I wake up in the next morning, hearing Caitlynn chitter chatter to her babies. Thankfully, she is feeling better, and I don't feel any different today. I'm still a mom, a wife, a nurse, and a woman. Only now, I have cancer growing inside of me. As I watch my daughter eat her toast, it makes me realize I can do this.

I have seven days, before I have a major operation and then start chemo. I have so much to do before this. Oh, my God. I still haven't told Carly and Carson yet. I haven't told anyone, except Maddox. I feel like I'm drifting along in the ocean, when I feel him wrap his arms around me. That is the exact moment I feel grounded. I feel safe and sure I'm going to be okay.

Turning around in his arms, I softly kiss him and tell him, "Thank you." He looks at me with questions on his face, but I just shake my head and place it on his chest. We stand like that for a few minutes, then I realize it's quiet. Looking around the corner, we see Caitlynn sleeping on the floor. She looks just like an angel sleeping there. Maddox goes to put her in her bed, as the phone rings.

It's Carly. I explain to her about the family meeting Monday, and she agrees to be here. We talk for a few more minutes, but she sounds preoccupied, so I assume she wants to get back with Xavier.

Hanging up, I turn to Maddox, "Let's just be a normal family this weekend."

"Whatever you want, babe. Would you do something with me? I want us to get matching tattoos. I believe we should get an anchor, since we've kept each other anchored. Maybe with our anniversary date on it?"

"Yes, I think we can manage that. I'll make our appointment."

We spend the weekend doing family things together. I'm nervous about telling the kids Monday, but I know it has to be done.

Claire

It's Sunday night, and we have had an awesome weekend together. I need to shower, so Maddox helps me upstairs. When I'm done, he wraps me up in a towel and dries me off. I head off to bed, and I think I'm asleep, before my head hits the pillow. Suddenly, I hear some pounding on the door. Stumbling around, I find some pants and one of Maddox's shirts, as I head downstairs. Opening the door, I cannot believe who I'm seeing, as Colton stands on my front porch. I'm so flabbergasted I cannot even think of anything to say, except, "What the fuck are you doing here?"

"Baby, I've missed you, and I want another chance. I love you so much, and I was so dumb to leave you for Clarissa. I want our family to be whole again." I can't even form a thought, so I slam the door shut. Running back upstairs, I grab my phone and call Maddox. I have to leave a message, so I call Carly and Carson.

Carly gets here first, and I hear her shouting loudly at her dad, so I go outside to make sure it doesn't get out of hand. As soon as I step outside, I see Maddox's truck, flying down the road. Just the sight of his truck makes me truly believe that I'm going to be okay. He jumps out and walks straight up to me, wrapping his arms around me. Then I hear Carson yelling, and I ask Maddox, "When did he get here?"

"He followed me. We were meeting at the hospital and having lunch with our girl."

I hear Carly say to Colton, "Dad, I told you, after you blackmailed me this last time, that I was done with you, and I mean it. When Xavier and I get married, it will be Maddox walking me down the aisle. As a matter of fact, I'm not even inviting you. Listen and listen well. I'm done with you. You are dead to me." Now, I know why she's been acting different. *Fucking Colton.*

Carson steps in next, "Well, now you have managed, all on your own, to alienate all of your kids from your life. Any other life goals?"

"Well, not all of my kids. Clarissa says she is pregnant again."

"Oh, my God. Please tell me you're not here to give up this child, too. I cannot believe that you haven't gotten fixed yet."

"Listen, Clarissa doesn't love me, and I don't love her. We can have our family back." He has to be high. I mean, no one is this stupid.

"Colton, I need you to listen, and this is the last time I ever want to see you again. I'm divorced

from you for a reason. You wanted everyone but me,
and I deserve better than that. I found a man that
loves me for me. I also just found out that I have
cancer, and guess what, he's still here by my side.
You would have run as far and as fast as you could
have. I hope you find someone that loves you the
way I love Maddox, and he loves me."

"I can take care of you. I love you, and I want
our family back."

"You're not listening to me. What we had was
an illusion. It wasn't real, because if it were, I would
feel something right now towards you, but I feel
absolutely nothing. Now, I can see my kids have a lot
of questions for me. So, for the final time, I don't
want to see you ever again. If I do, I will get a
restraining order on you."

"Can I see Caitlynn?"

This guy just doesn't get it. "No! You signed
all your rights away, as if she were a car. She doesn't
know you, and she never will. Maddox and I are her
parents now. Carly and Carson come on in, so I can

explain this." Still holding Maddox's hand, we walk into the house and close the door.

With a sigh, I drop my head to his chest, "Well, that didn't go over like I thought. I had hoped to break it to the kids gently."

He softly kisses my head, "It will be okay. We have each other and the kids."

"You make me believe in myself, and in us. I don't know what I did that was so great to get you, but I'm so thankful for that, and every second I have you." I kiss his lips softly, and neither of us move, until we hear a throat clearing behind us.

Walking together to the chair, he sits down and puts me in his lap, as we begin explaining everything that has happened to the kids. It's hard to get through, but with Maddox by my side, I feel as though I can get through anything.

"Mom, how did you get this?" Carly asks crying.

"I don't know, and the doctors don't know. However, it is only stage two, so I'll be okay, I promise."

"Are you going to die?" Carson asks, losing his battle with the tears.

"I promise you right now I will do everything in my power to fight this and win. I can't tell you that I'll live forever because we all know that would be a lie. What I can promise is to fight, as hard as I can."

Carly walks out of the room, and I start to freak out, thinking she is having a breakdown. I should have known better, because about three minutes later, she comes back in and tells me she has a bath drawn for me, and she will make dinner for everyone.

She turns, asking, "How did Molly and Frank take the news?"

"I told you I haven't told anyone, except you kids and Maddox." I turn around to get undressed, and I hear her sniffle. I wrap my arms around her and hold her tight, while she cries it out. *She is breaking my heart.*

"I don't want you to die. Can't God just take me and leave you here?"

"Carly Lynn, it would destroy me, if anything ever happened to you. I'm a fighter. Plus, I have you, Carson, Caitlynn, Xavier, and Maddox to live for. I can promise you I will not give up without a fight."

"I love you."

"Baby girl, I love you more than you will ever know." She nods her head and walks out. I drain the bath and just start the shower, while I sit on the floor and cry.

I cry for the pain my kids are feeling. I cry for the unfairness of the situation. I cry because Caitlynn is so young, and she isn't going to understand that Mommy is too sick to play, or why I will be bald. I don't know how long I sat in there and cry, before I feel Maddox wrap me in his arms, until I finally quit crying.

Gently but firmly, he grips my chin, so I look at him, "Babe, you're stronger than this, but when you feel like you're not strong enough, can you let me be the strength you need? We'll be perfect together, and I will be right beside you the whole time. Nothing will stop me from being with you every step of the way. I need you to believe in me, as much as I do."

"I promise, my love. I will let you be the strength I need, when I don't have it."

He lets out a breath I didn't realize he was holding. "I've got you, babe."

******

The next morning everyone is already gone, so I throw on some clothes, heading downstairs to just relax. My boss called earlier, saying my shifts are covered, so that's one less thing off my list.

As I sit on my porch, I decide I need to do something, so I go to the local greenhouse and buy a truck bed full of flowers, and then start planting. I had no idea digging in the dirt, and matching flowers in the flower beds was so much of a stress reliever. I have gone all around the porch, when I realize that I have been out in the sun all day and only had a bagel to eat. I can't be upset because my house looks so pretty, and I did it.

I'm walking back to the house from the shed, when I hear the truck pull in. Caitlynn sees me first, and she takes off running. It takes me a minute, but I realize she has on her Christmas dress, which is green and gold with blue leggings with skulls all over them. "Mommy! Look, Daddy let me dress myself today. Everybody at daycare said how awesome I look!" Bending down, as she launches herself at me, so I can catch her, I laugh.

"I bet they did because you are so awesome. I love you. What did you do at daycare today?"

She starts talking a mile a minute, explaining every single part of her day. When she finally stops, I say, "That's so awesome. I'm glad you had a good day. Want to see what I did today? I just know you're going to love it. Look at all the pretty flowers I planted." Her whole face lights up.

Letting her down, so she can inspect all the flowers, Maddox comes over, wrapping his arms around me. "Babe, I'm not sure I want the kids to stay here. I know they want to be close, and if I'm really sick, or you have to work, that is fine. But they have their own lives they need to live."

"I understand both sides, so you're going to have to talk to them about it, when they come over for dinner tonight. We need to pack our bags for the hospital, so we can be there right at four forty- five tomorrow morning. I can almost guarantee that they will stay tonight and miss class tomorrow."

It Begins with Goodbye

"What are we going to tell Caitlynn?"

"She knows something is going on. She is smart. We're going to tell her that you have something in your belly that the doctors have to take out. That you're going to spend the night at the hospital, and then you will be home with us Saturday."

Turning in his arms, I wrap mine around his neck, "I was headed back to the house from the shed, when I heard your truck, and I stopped at the corner and just watched you. I thought to myself my God he is mine, and you can bet your sweet ass I'm not giving him up without a fight. I love you, babe." He reaches down, kissing me sweetly, and it's moments like this that make everything better.

Later that night, Carson still hasn't shown up at the house for dinner; and it's starting to worry me. He has a need to fix everything for everyone, but he doesn't handle stuff good himself. I tell everyone I'll be back, as I head to the place I know I will find him at the local football field. When I get there, he sits just as I suspected at the fifty-yard line, and I don't make a sound, as I climb the bleachers and sit next to him. I also don't make a sound, when his head lands on my lap, or when my pants are wet from his tears. I still don't make a sound, when he wraps his arms around me, but when the sobs rip out of his chest, that is when mine start.

I don't know how long we sit here holding each other and crying. Finally, he asks the questions that he wants, and I'm honest with him, explaining what I know. I have never kept things from my kids, and they have been there, when no one else has. I have always asked for honesty from everyone including them, and in return, they get it back from me. Sometimes, they don't like what I have to say, but they can bet their last dollar it's one hundred percent honest.

"Can I skip the family dinner tonight, so I can come to terms with everything?" I agree because everyone deals differently. We walk down the bleachers together, and there stands Maddox, Caitlynn, Carly, and Xavier holding a picnic basket.

Carson wraps his arms around me, and whispers, "I'll be there in the morning. I love you." He walks over and kisses Carly on her forehead and gives a fist bump to Xavier and Maddox.

However, Caitlynn isn't having any of that, as she launches herself at him, wrapping her arms and legs around him. They whisper back and forth for a few minutes, before turning and walking over to us, grabbing the basket, and then walking to the end zone. Guess he is staying for her. I love the bond between all of my children. We eat and talk, and enjoy this time together, as a family.

Finally, it's time to go home, and I'm emotionally exhausted. I take Caitlynn in, and we are singing, as I give her a bath and get ready for bed. I sit and rock with her longer than necessary, but how long will it be, before I can do this again? Finally, I lay her in her bed, when I hear the front door open. I go downstairs, and there in the middle of my front room is Carly, Carson, Xavier, and Maddox waiting for me.

Carson says, "Mom, can I spend the night with you?"

"Us too?" Carly asks.

I can't do anything but laugh. "Of course, you guys can stay, but I need you three to promise me something though. I need you to promise to continue to live your lives. I will let you go with me to treatments and doctor's appointments, but we all need to try and be as normal as possible, okay?"

"I can promise you that, but I can also promise anytime I need to see you, or Maddox tells me you're sick or need anything, I'll be here. Please don't argue because you would do the same for us. We love you and are only doing what you do, when you love someone."

"Okay, I can deal with that." I finally agree with Carly. They really believe they have just won, when in reality, that is all I wanted from the beginning.

It Begins with Goodbye

Finally, Maddox and I make it to our room, and I lay in his arms just enjoying the feeling of his heart beating strong and steady, under my head. After a while, I get out of bed and pack my bags. "Babe, what are you doing out of bed?"

"Oh, my God! You scared the crap out of me." I jump, slapping my hand to my chest. "I couldn't sleep, so I packed my stuff and was just going over the list in my head, and then I was going to get back in bed."

"Come on. We can get everything in a couple hours. I want to spend as much time as I can with you, and inside of you." We slowly make love, and it's not just with our body's though, but it's our hearts and souls.

******

The next morning, I'm awake, before the alarm clock goes off, so I just lay in bed, watching Maddox sleep. It's moments like this that I don't want to lose.

After everyone is dressed, and we drop Caitlynn off at daycare, the kids and Maddox escort me to the third floor to the surgical wing. They settle in, while I go about checking in and getting ready for surgery. Once I have my IV in and am in my lovely gown, they come in to see me.

The doctor comes in and talks to everyone, answering any questions they have. Once they start giving me the good drugs, you know the ones that knock you out, I'm literally floating on cloud nine. The kids give me kisses and hugs and head to the waiting room.

"Carly, please bring Caitlynn up to see me tonight," I say, and she quickly agrees.

Finally, it's Maddox and I alone. I pat the bed next to me, and he lays down, as I place my head on his heart.

"What is your favorite sound?"

"The beat of your heart."

"What is your favorite thing to look at?"

"Your smile."

"What is your favorite thing to do?"

"Anything with you."

"What is your favorite smell?"

"You."

"Do you have any idea how much I love you?"

"Umm, since I love you more, yeah I think I do." Chuckling he kisses me, "Babe, go to sleep, and I'll be here, when you come back." I don't feel him leave the bed, and the next thing I know some lady is telling me to wake up. All at once I feel him slide under me, as I smell him and hear his heartbeat. At that moment, I feel safe and secure, and I know that everything will be okay.

R.S. James

Epilogue

5 years later

Today marks the five-year anniversary of me being diagnosed with ovarian cancer. We also celebrated Caitlynn's eighth birthday last weekend. Today is also the day I find out if the cancer is gone for good, or if I need more treatment. I have Maddox and the kids with me today, and I know in my heart of hearts that I wouldn't be who and where I am today without their love and support.

I have a picture on my phone of when I woke up after my hysterectomy, and Carly is laying on Xavier's lap, both sleeping on the couch in my room. Carson is in the chair with Caitlynn on his lap asleep. Maddox is laid on the bed right next to me, and in that moment, I knew what unconditional love was. The kids still say Maddox and I act like teenagers, instead of parents, but why keep our hands to ourselves, when we don't have to? I believe that sometimes you must go through the bad to get to the good. I'm not saying that everything with Colton was bad, but it wasn't always good either. Maddox and I don't always see eye to eye, but I know without a shadow of a doubt that he will never cheat or break my heart.

We haven't heard any more from Colton, since he found out I was completely done. Clarissa still hasn't even tried to see Caitlynn or any of us. Carly and Xavier are doing well, and I hope in a year or so to have a wedding to attend. Carson is still Carson. He has found the one, but he isn't admitting it yet. He tells everyone he doesn't have room in his life for another girl, since Caitlynn has stolen his heart. He told me once that he is afraid to get to attached to a girl for fear he is his father's son. I tried to knock that thought right out of his head, and I told him that is not something that is handed down. If you truly love someone, then you have no reason to cheat.

We are all holding hands, as we wait for the doctor to come in with the news. Finally, the door opens, and the doctor walks in, while looking at a chart. I take a deep breath and look at everyone in this room with me, and I know I'm okay. Looking at the doctor, I say, "Regardless of the results today, I'm perfect."

He nods his head, "Yes Claire, you are, and you are still in remission. You won't need tested for another five years. Congratulations."

Everyone is whooping, as I sit with tears rolling down my face. Maddox looks at me, "Babe, why are you crying? This is amazing news."

"We fought, and we won! We beat it."

"No babe, you did this."

"No Maddox, if it weren't for you and our kids, I would've had nothing to fight for and no one to fight beside me. So yes, we did it." I kiss him with all of the emotions I have in me. This has been the greatest news, since finding Maddox.

It Begins with Goodbye

R.S. James

THE END

About the Author

R.S. James is an up and coming romance author and an avid reader. First, I am a mom to two active kids who keep this sports mom hopping from one event to the other, and the wife to a hunter and fisherman who enjoys spending time with his family.

I'm a big believer in family and I love being a sister, an aunt, and a daughter. I enjoy sitting on the porch enjoying talking with my friends who I hold close to my heart.

The voices of my characters demanded that their stories come to life so now here I am letting you in on my the going ins and outs of my mind.

R.S. James

Made in the USA
Monee, IL
21 July 2022

10093207R00164